Bridge to London

heart
capital
books

DEDICATION

To those who are waiting to blossom.

"And the day came when the risk to remain tight in a bud
was more painful than the risk it took to blossom."
Anais Nin

ACKNOWLEDGMENTS

To my friends—thank you for holding me up when I couldn't stand on my own, for listening when I needed to vent, and for reminding me of my worth when I forgot. Your love, encouragement, and unwavering belief in me carried me through the hardest moments. I poured my heart into these pages, but it was your hearts that gave me the strength to finish. I will never forget it.

CONTENTS

CHAPTER 1

London Henderson stepped inside the posh restaurant at exactly five pm, even though she knew that her best friend would be late to arrive at their agreed upon time. She was immediately surrounded by warmth, and was glad to be out of the crisp February cold. Rubbing her hands together to warm them, she again wondered where she had left her gloves.

Before she could dwell on it, the couple in front of her stepped to the side and the host greeted her. She let him know that she would wait for the rest of her reservation and walked the short distance to the bar.

Seated in the center of the restaurant, the bar was anchored to the ceiling, and its canopy was framed in a hodgepodge of wooden shutters that should have looked odd.

Instead, the theme was carried throughout the restaurant, with shutters lining the ceiling and strategically placed white curtains to separate parts of the space. It had a home-like dining room setting that somehow felt uniquely upscale.

She chose a pair of soft, taupe colored chairs at the end of the bar and shrugged out of her black pea coat before sitting. Accepting the drink menu with a small smile, London angled her chair toward the entrance, content to fill the time with people watching.

Gianna Maffuci was consistently, and fashionably, late, while London was consistently on time. She didn't begrudge her friend, and instead appreciated the last bit of quiet that she would have for the next few hours.

Their friend Valerie Hall would marry her gorgeous hunk of a man, Jun Kobayashi, in just two months and so the couple had invited the wedding party to Ella Dining Room and Bar for a bit of a pre-wedding who's who celebration.

In the year since their engagement, London had gotten to know Jun's dental partner, Dustin Pierce, and had met his sister, Mika, a handful of times. Everyone else was a stranger despite the wedding party being small.

Since they had planned a destination wedding, she would be spending a lot more time with Jun's friends and family than she would at a typical wedding. She appreciated having an opportunity to meet them before they left for a week in Hawaii.

London ordered a glass of red wine and returned her attention to the door. Watching people come and go, she made up names and stories about them for her own personal entertainment. An odd pastime for sure, but it was something she had been doing most of her life.

She didn't always enjoy being the center of attention, preferring to blend in and observe whenever she could. Her looks, however, often belied this desire.

At five seven, London was tall and thin, a product of biology more than anything else in her opinion. Her black hair was cut in a tapered style, leaving her small oval shaped face open for view. For much of her life, friends and strangers alike told her she had the look and body of a model.

London considered herself average looking at best, and always believed that her body and bone structure was what led people to insist that she pursue a career in modeling. Added to that, she never enjoyed getting attention for her looks, so that life never seemed like the right fit for her.

The idea of using her looks and body to get and stay in the limelight seemed terribly exhausting to her. She never tried to hide her body behind oversized clothing or anything like that, but she preferred getting dolled up for her own personal pleasure, not because it was her job.

So she had chosen a career that often left many people surprised, and sometimes a little impressed. But she wasn't a Client's Right Advocate at Disability Rights California for the accolades. She liked helping people because she thought it was the right thing to do.

London perked up a bit, distracted from her thoughts when two attractive men walked in. Hot Harry and Sexy Suit, she decided instantly.

Hot Harry had short, thick brunette hair that bounced and swayed with him whenever he moved. His short beard was immaculately cut and did absolutely nothing to hide the dimples that winked out against his pale skin.

Bright, blue eyes looked at Sexy Suit with a smirk as they approached the bar. He was dressed in red sweats and a gray tattered hooded sweatshirt, which completely confused her since Sexy Suit was, obviously, wearing a suit.

And boy was he wearing it. The black casual suit was tailored perfectly to his body, and highlighted his broad shoulders and slim figure.

His black hair was just long enough to need to be kept off his forehead with hair product, and it's length continued to fade shorter and shorter as it reached his temples.

Unlike Hot Harry, his face was clean-shaven, so when he returned the smirk to his friend, there was nothing to hide its power.

She hated that she was immediately attracted to him. She had sworn off dating Asian men years ago, and Hot Harry was the type of guy she now tried to gravitate to. Tried being the key word.

But she was an absolute sucker for a man in a suit, and even when she realized he was watching her watching him, she couldn't look away.

They stared at each other in open curiosity until he turned, his attention drawn to Gianna as she fluttered in noisily.

"I am soo sorry," she said as she made her way to London.

London shifted her focus away from Sexy Suit and stood to hug her friend.

"You're only fifteen minutes late. I'm impressed."

Gianna smiled and took her coat off, looking casually over her shoulder.

"I'd say my timing was perfect. Did you see those guys?"

London chuckled. "You don't miss anything do you?"

"I saw them walk up while I was waiting to cross the street, but the view from here is so much better. The guy in the hoodie," she said dramatically. "So rugged."

"I wanted to talk to Hot Harry," London said, frowning at Gianna as she ordered a drink.

Gianna slid another look at Hot Harry, saw that he was watching her.

"Oh, honey. He's too short for you, and you can't tell me that the guy in the suit didn't get your juices going."

She picked up her drink to hide her scowl. "You know I don't date Asian guys anymore."

"What did you call Hot Harry's friend?" Gianna slanted her a look, waiting patiently for the answer, though she could guess what it was.

Now she pouted. "Sexy Suit."

"Of course!" Gianna said with a laugh. "So why not find out if he's as sexy without the suit on and then ghost him afterwards?"

"That's fucked up."

Gianna shrugged. "I really don't think Hot Harry will mind when I do it to him."

"You're kind of a mess, you know that?"

Gianna rolled her eyes. "No, I just know how to play the game. Now, who's going to the bathroom?"

London sighed, knowing it was futile to argue. "Can we at least do a quick toast to your first week at Intel? That is why we came here so early after all."

"You're cute when you stall," Gianna said with a grin, but held her glass up anyway. "There's nothing to toast to. It's just a job."

"At a multinational technological corporation that requires what I consider a genius level knowledge of math and computers. But you're right, no big deal."

"Exactly!" She tapped her glass to London's and then took a sip. "Who's going?"

London took a final sip. "I'll go. I'm sure Hot Harry is anxious to touch the flame."

Gianna grinned wickedly. "Burn, baby, burn."

London stood up and looked over at the men. Hot Harry was too busy stealing glances at Gianna to notice, but she saw Sexy Suit's eyes flick toward her for a brief moment before he looked away.

Walking to the bathroom, she wondered if she would get burned too, because despite her weak protests, she did want to talk to Sexy Suit.

Inside the bathroom, she took her time touching up her makeup, delaying the inevitable. Annoyed with herself, she forced herself to set aside her bias. Not all Asian men were like her ex.

And she wasn't even looking for anything serious. It was just going to be a little harmless flirting to pass the time until dinner.

Seated at the bar, Tony reminded himself that it was just going to be a little harmless flirting to pass the time until dinner. He watched for the ebony goddess to return, taking a sip of his beer to calm his nerves as he waited. He was still just a little bit dazed from when he had first seen her. There had been something so honest and appealing on that oval shaped face.

And she had been looking at him, openly assessing him as if the instant attraction he had felt was mutual.

A punch of heat hit him dead in the chest as she stepped into the dining space. She wore an orange long sleeved dress with some sort of black pattern dancing across it. A thick, black belt cinched the dress at her waist, highlighting her figure and drawing his attention to the tasteful display of cleavage it revealed.

Her hips swayed gently as she walked to the bar, her eyes passing over the man who had taken her seat to talk to her friend. Then her eyes zeroed in on him. He let out a small breath as she approached him.

Tony stood, gestured to the empty seat next to him. "Do you want to sit? I'm sure my friend will make an ass of himself shortly and you can get back to yours. Can I get you a drink in the meantime?"

London eased into the chair. "A glass of red would be nice."

Tony sat and lifted a hand to get the bartender's attention. After she ordered, he angled his body towards hers to face her.

"I'm Tony. My friend drooling all over yours is Oliver."

"I'm London, and that's Gianna. She's used to drool."

"I imagine this type of thing happens to the two of you very often."

"What type of thing?" She gladly accepted her drink and took a small sip.

"Guys interrupting your night with your friend to hit on you," he clarified, shifting his weight to retrieve his card from his wallet. He passed it to the bartender. "I'll take another beer. You can start a tab."

"It's certainly a first for a guy to be so blatant about trying to get me drunk."

"What?" He turned so quickly that he nearly knocked over his beer. He righted it with both hands before it spilled. "I'm not...that's not what I meant."

When she only laughed in response, he hoped it was safe to assume that she was joking. Still, he felt the back of his neck heat up in embarrassment. He slipped his wallet back in his pocket.

"The tab is for me. I've got some time to kill before dinner. You're welcome to get whatever you want, of the nonalcoholic variety, since we interrupted your ladies night."

London lifted her eyebrow. "Did it not occur to you that maybe we interrupted your guys time?"

He blinked. "What do you mean?"

London smiled, and then crossed her legs so she could lean back in the chair. "I mean, maybe Gianna and I are exactly where we want to be."

His eyes tracked the movement of her legs before he snapped them back to her face. "Oh, yeah, that sounds right. Two of the most beautiful women I've ever seen, decided to give chase after seeing Oliver, in his sweaty shorts, and me in my…well I guess I do look like I belong in here."

"So being beautiful means I can't go after what I want?" She asked, inclining her head in consideration.

"You should absolutely always go after what you want," he answered quietly, warmed by the idea that she could possibly want him. "It just seems to me that chasing men shouldn't be something either one of you need to do. Batting them off? Wiping off unwanted drool? Giving out fake numbers? Absolutely necessary for your survival."

London took another sip of wine. "You sound as though you're speaking from experience, though I thought men like having women chase them."

He laughed, sitting back in his chair and relaxing a little. "Women don't chase me, but I have been given the wrong number a time or two."

"Oh yeah, that sounds right," she said, mimicking what he had said before.

Tony just looked at her. Their eyes locked, and the space around them grew still and quiet, heavy with the weight of his attraction. And maybe, if he wasn't seeing something that he wanted to see, the weight of her attraction to him.

For a moment, he let himself believe that she was his. For this moment anyway, he could have her. Not wanting it to end, he committed her face to his memory.

She didn't understand why he was watching her that way, or why it made her heart race and left her speechless. There was heat in his brown eyes that spoke of his desire, but there was something else there that she didn't recognize.

She wanted to find out what it was. She hoped he would let her. Though he encouraged her to always go after what she wanted, and usually she did, she promised herself that she would approach men like him with extreme caution.

They sat quietly like that for a few minutes, both absently sipping their beverages while they assessed each other, wondering if the other would take the leap.

"So," she said quietly, finally breaking the silence. "Why are you the only one in a suit, Tony?"

God he liked the way she said his name. "Oliver and I were supposed to play ball over at CalFit, but we didn't have enough people, and didn't feel like playing one on one. I'm meeting some friends here for dinner tonight so we decided to get a drink here instead. What about you?"

"Same."

He smirked. "You were playing ball at CalFit?"

"Haha. I'm also meeting friends for dinner," she responded dryly. "I have no basketball skills whatsoever. I prefer to watch it."

"Who is your favorite team?"

London sighed a little, bracing herself for the usual reaction. "The Kings."

"Oh, yeah? Mine too."

She narrowed her eyes at him. "Are you serious?"

Tony laughed. "Yes."

"Prove it," she demanded, unconvinced.

"Only if you can."

London tried not to smile as she uncrossed her legs and moved her purse into her lap. She could feel his eyes on her as she pulled out her phone from inside.

"You might want to pull up some proof too," she suggested.

He grinned and retrieved his own phone. Tony knew that he could prove his fan boy status with his business card, but wasn't quite ready to reveal that little tidbit of information just yet.

"See?"

She held up a photo from her Instagram. In it she wore a white jersey with Kings displayed in purple across her chest. He could tell from the background that she was at a game. He also tried to commit her user name to his memory incase he was desperate enough to look her up on the platform later.

"Alright. Okay. I see you're at the Golden 1 Center so I know it's a recent photo."

"That's right. Where is your proof?"

She leaned forward, and he did the same. He felt his body heat in response as he held out his phone to show her the photo of him and Slamson, the Kings mascot, in front of the Golden 1 Center.

London grinned, and thought he looked equally good in a jacket and jeans.

"Look at that goofy grin. You're a fan all right. Shocker."

"I see I'm not the only one who gets crazy looks when I say I'm a Kings fan."

"Yes!" she shouted, feeling vindicated. "We're supposed to be Lakers or Warriors fans."

"Pft. No thanks." He scrunched up his face to convey his disgust. "I've been a fan since I was ten, and I never miss a game if I can help it."

London grinned. "I haven't managed that, but I do watch it when I can. How do you feel about the team being at the Golden1 Center?"

He smiled, wondering again if he should share just how much time he spent in the team's new arena.

"I know a lot of people were worried about it being downtown, but I think it works. Sure it makes the space a little more cramped, but it's still better than Arco."

London placed a hand over her heart and pretended to wipe away tears with the other. "And you still call the original arena Arco."

Tony grinned. "I don't care what they rename the old arena, it will always be Arco Arena to me."

"Absolutely! I honestly don't even know what they're calling it now."

"Doesn't matter."

"I was invited to attend a game in a few weeks. Some fundraiser deal for my job. I may have to go."

Excited by the prospect of seeing her again, he bit his tongue rather than suggest he meet her there. He could feel a dark cloud settling over his head as he realized he should pull back. But he couldn't bring himself to do it just yet.

Curious about her thoughts, and appreciating the fact that he could have an avid conversation about the team with a true fan, he asked her about her favorite players. This took them down the rabbit hole of past players, close games, and their loss of the championship. They even spent some time talking about The Sacramento Monarchs, the city's former WNBA team.

This was a first for him, Tony realized. He had met plenty of women who loved sports, but he had never had more than a passing interest in them. Knowing that he and London shared this interest only made him want her more. Realizing he was slipping into dangerous ground, he switched gears.

"Since you're a Kings fan, I'm guessing that you're from Sacramento."

"Yep. Born and raised, though I left for undergrad. This place pulled me back. Same for you?"

"The raised part, yeah, but I was born in San Francisco and moved here when I was in elementary school."

London smiled. "I imagine we've crossed paths a time or two then."

"Possibly. Probably. You strike me as too cool to frequent the places I haunt. That's meant to be a compliment."

She lifted an eyebrow. "Oh? What places are those?"

"Well, let's just say that a lot of people say I act more like I'm in my early twenties rather than my early thirties."

"And that means?"

"I'm no stranger to bars and clubs."

"Ah, so you're a wild one. And you don't think I am."

"Everyone has a little wild in them. You just give

off this vibe that you're above all of that. You're not about to waste your wild on just anyone. Classy woman like you…you're waiting on the right person."

The look in his eyes made her think that he hoped to be the right person. Or maybe that's what she wanted to see.

"I like bars and clubs," she replied, not knowing what else to say.

"Do you go every weekend?"

She blinked at him. "Do you?"

"Just about."

She laughed. "That sounds awful."

He frowned into his glass. "It's not that bad."

"I like going out. I like the music, the energy, and the anonymous company of strangers. But every weekend? What are you looking for?"

You, he thought. And because he wanted to tell her, he knew that he needed to stop this before he did something he couldn't take back. He got the bartender's attention so he could close his tab.

"Nothing that complicated, I swear. I guess I just unwind better with all that music, energy, and the anonymous company of strangers, as you put it."

London shook her head, a small and confused smile on her face. Then he pulled out his wallet and phone, looking at the screen briefly before shoving it back in his pocket.

"My friend is here. I have to go." Tony sighed, then put his card back in his wallet, and forced himself to do the complete opposite of what he wanted to do.

He slid off the chair quickly, pushing it in. Refusing to look at her, the words tumbled out of his mouth.

"It was really, really, really great talking to you, London. You take care."

Needing a moment, he walked out of the restaurant, refusing to look back. Ignoring the insistent pressure on his heart that demanded he go back, he sucked in the cool February air and wiped his hands over his face.

God he hoped that he wouldn't see her across the restaurant once they were seated. He wasn't sure he trusted himself to behave.

Because as much as he wanted to worship London like the queen she surely was, he absolutely couldn't have her. They could never be together.

∞∞∞∞∞∞∞∞

"What do you mean he ghosted you?"

London tugged Gianna closer to her. "Will you keep your voice down?"

Enraged, Gianna looked around to see if anyone had heard her before leaning closer. "What happened?"

"He ghosted me. Flirted with me that entire time, and then just got up and walked out of the restaurant."

"And he didn't ask for your number?"

"Nope."

Gianna sat back in her chair. "That fucking bastard."

"Yeah, that."

"I'm sorry, London," she said, rubbing London's arm.

London shook her head. "Don't be. He didn't mean anything. And now you see why I don't date Asian guys anymore."

"Ugh."

They sat at the end of a long table in Ella's elegant private dining room. The walls were a backdrop of rose gold and were enhanced with large gold utensils that were painted on them. The same velvety taupe chairs surrounded the table and were slowly being filled up with Valerie and Jun's family and friends.

So far the only new faces she saw were who she assumed were Jun's parents. The room only seated fourteen, and was filling up quickly.

"Oh my gawd," Gianna gasped.

"What?"

London looked up to see what Gianna was gawking at and saw Tony and Jun embracing in a brief man hug. She felt a kind of knowing in the air, as if her body was alerting her that he was near.

She knew he must have felt it too because his body language changed, and his eyes swept across the room until they focused solely on her. They widened in complete surprise and the ready smile on his face faltered as he was pulled away to greet the others.

"He's friends with Jun? Do you think Val set you guys up?"

London shook her head. "No. He wouldn't have looked so surprised if she had put him up to this."

Gianna scowled at him. "What are you going to do?"

"Nothing. I told you, he didn't mean anything."

"Are you sure about that? Shit, Jun is bringing him over here."

London stood to embrace Jun. "Hello, handsome."

"Hey, London. Gianna. Wow," he added, as he looked them over. His mouth dropped open comically and he used his hands to close it. "As always, you ladies look absolutely jaw-droppingly gorgeous."

Gianna grinned, and there was something a little bit malicious in it. "You're so funny, Jun. And who is this?"

"This is Tony. Tony, this is London and Gianna. Valerie's besties."

"Tony. Nice to meet you," London said, holding out her hand for him to shake.

Having memorized her face, Tony already knew that the smile she gave him was fake. And though he felt a bolt of electricity the moment he took her hand, she offered him a weak handshake.

He had to tamp down the quick and irrational desire to drop to his feet and beg for her forgiveness. Gianna, on the other hand, dug her nails in his hand just enough to let him know that he was on her shit list.

Exactly where he deserved to be.

"Nice to meet you too," he said weakly.

Fuck, shit, damnit, he thought, as Jun led him away to meet everyone else. *Fuck, fuck, fucking fuck fuck.*

The rest of the dinner passed by in a fog as he cursed himself, and his luck. Seated at the opposite end and side of the table, he could see her beautiful face as she observed the crowd, a small smile on her face. She spoke infrequently and never to him.

Rightfully so, she was ignoring him completely. She didn't so much as look at him, only glancing in his general direction to talk to Dustin, who was seated next to him.

And it was killing him. It killed him to see and want her, to know that they couldn't be together. It killed him to know that she probably hated him now, and he absolutely deserved it.

As dinner finally began to wind down, he debated on lingering a bit. The night probably promised a lot more suffering whether he stayed or went home. Too miserable to be any kind of decent company, he decided to call it a night.

He said his goodbyes, risking one last look at London as he made his way out. She still wouldn't look at him.

Damn, he thought as he headed for the bathroom. If only she would let him explain. But what could he say? My parents will kill me if I don't date a Chinese girl?

Even if it was true, it didn't explain why he had sat there for nearly an hour, brazenly flirting with her. He could tell her that he wanted her, but what would be the point? And why did it feel like he was trying to explain his own behavior to himself?

Disgusted with himself, Tony made his way out of the restaurant. When he got outside, she was standing near the valet as if she had been waiting for him. He told himself not to, but his body betrayed him and moved toward her of its own will.

"London."

Bundled up in her coat, London turned slightly in his direction. Her eyes passed over him quickly, dismissing him, before she turned back.

"Tony."

He preferred the way she said his name that first time. There was too much malice in her voice now.

"I guess we'll be seeing a lot of each other after all."

"I guess so."

The air filled with the sounds of the city at night as he just kept staring at her, making her feel uncomfortable.

Annoyed, she shot him a glare. "Is there something you need?"

"Yes," he responded quickly, his voice low and dark.

London turned to face him, and saw it clearly now. The barely restrained desire. It made the air around him crackle. Her eyes narrowed in response.

Vibrating with fury, she clenched her hands into fists, surprised by how much she wanted to strike him. She didn't understand, and didn't want to understand what was holding him back. That was his problem, not hers, and she didn't want anything to do with him.

Her phone vibrated in her pocket, signaling her rideshare had arrived, just as a car pulled up behind her. Without a word, she turned and climbed inside. When she dared look back, he was still standing on the street, watching her.

CHAPTER 2

She had amazing friends.

London had bonded with Valerie and Gianna on their first day of high school. Young, excited, and just a little bit afraid of the new journey, they found each other, and had been all but inseparable ever since.

She remembered that day clearly, and all the awkward nerves she had felt.

Valerie had given her a shy smile as she made her way onto the bus in Lincoln Village, the neighborhood where they had grown up. She had smiled in return before withdrawing inside herself to watch and observe all of the new faces.

And she had sat there, quiet and content, until Gianna. It wasn't until the bus had picked up Gianna in Rosemont that the circle had formed. Gianna, always the extrovert, had plopped down beside her and immediately started talking a mile a minute.

She remembered how Gianna had glowed and vibrated with anticipation, her brunette locks curling around her beautiful face. She drew quite a bit of attention to herself, as she would quickly learn was usual, but she kept her attention focused on her new friend.

It wasn't long before she looped Valerie and her

cousin Hunter, who were sitting behind them, into the conversation. Poor Hunter, a year older and twice as shy, had merely stared at her in wonder.

The three of them did basically everything together from that moment forward. School clubs, sports, studying, dances, shopping, and whatever classes they could get in together.

It wasn't until they had gone off to college, with each one attending a different school throughout the state, that the trio went solo. Despite the distance, they managed to keep in contact, touching base with each other for birthdays and holidays. London had even managed to connect with Valerie a few times in Southern California.

When London had moved back to Sacramento for graduate school, she and Gianna started getting together again. And when Valerie moved back, they rebuilt that same friendship that they had formed in high school.

It was because of their friendship, and the promise of bottomless mimosas, that she tolerated this unnecessary inquisition into last night's events.

Cafeteria 15L had an eclectic and industrial feel with its hodgepodge of tables and chairs and exposed metal beams. It was a popular spot for weekend brunch, and today was no exception.

London wasn't sure how Gianna had managed to get a reservation, but since she didn't envy the line of people waiting outside, she didn't question it. She scanned the faces of the people around her, sipping her mimosa, as Gianna filled Valerie in on what happened.

"Wow. I can't believe he ghosted you," Valerie said, pushing her wine glass forward for more.

Gianna gladly filled her glass, adding more

champagne than orange juice. "I know, right! How dense is this guy?"

London merely rolled her eyes and continued sipping her drink, feeling that this was more about the gossip and scandal than anything else.

"He's only come around a handful of times in the last year. Jun says he's always busy with work and helps his parents out sometimes with their shop or restaurant? I'm not sure which one it is."

"Sounds like he must be single then," Gianna inferred, pouring another drink for herself.

Valerie shrugged. "I don't know. I know whenever Jun does go out to bars, it's usually with Tony and his friends."

"Ugh, Val. You're supposed to be supplying me with all the deets!"

Valerie laughed. "Sorry! Let me think back. Well, I thought I offended him when I first met him. And since then, he has always struck me as shy or standoffish. I haven't been around him enough to figure out which one it is."

London shook her head. "You guys do realize I would have ghosted him eventually even if I had given him my actual number, and not a fake one."

"Really?" Valerie asked, surprised.

"I told you I don't do Asian guys anymore."

Gianna scrunched up her nose. "I hate when you say that. You can't treat all Asian men the same."

"Okay, fine." London stopped when the waiter appeared, preferring to let him finish serving their food before she continued.

"Oh, my gosh. This just looks amazing," Gianna said, beaming up at the waiter. "Thank you so much. I know that you're super busy, but could you please bring us some extra syrup? We'd really appreciate it."

"Ah, of course," he said, staring at her in awe. "I'll be right back with that."

"Thank you!" She called as he walked away. Then her sharp eyes zeroed back in on London. "You were saying?"

"I don't date Asian guys who don't ask me for my number."

"Not good enough!"

London shrugged. "It's going to have to be. Look, I don't know why Tony didn't ask for my number even though he seemed like he was really into me, but I can guess, from experience, what it might be. The whole thing reminded me too much of Elliot, and I'm not going to repeat that same mistake."

Valerie touched her arm. "What if he had asked for your number?"

"I would have given it to him. Maybe even have gone on a few dates, but I think I'd honestly be waiting for him to bail because I'm not Asian."

"Damn it, London," Gianna sighed, putting her fork down as if she had lost her appetite.

"And that's why I say I don't want to date Asian guys anymore. I can't build a relationship with someone I'm expecting will walk away."

"So change your expectations," Valerie suggested.

"Maybe one day I will, but it won't be with someone like Tony."

"What will you do when you see him again?" Gianna asked. "I mean, he is in the wedding."

"Maybe I should have Dustin walk with you down the aisle," Valerie considered.

"You guys are making a bigger deal out of this than it is. I thought the guy was cute, but he's not the first cute guy who didn't ask me for my number. It's not that serious. And once we're in Hawaii, he'll be the last thing on my mind."

Gianna pouted a bit. "Well I'm still going to be mean to him. That jerk."

"Same. Probably," Valerie added with a sheepish smile.

London grinned. "I am both appalled by and proud of you both."

"Chicks before dicks," Gianna announced.

Valerie held up her glass in agreement. "Chicks before dicks!"

Chuckling, London did the same, bumping her glass lightly against her friends. "Chicks before dicks."

She was still smiling about the entire exchange as she began the ten-minute walk to the Midtown Farmers Market. The market closed down 20th Street for two blocks between J and K Street, and had over fifty vendors selling fresh fruits and vegetables, specialty foods, and handcrafted goods.

She walked there every week, rain or shine, and thanks to on demand bike and scooter rental companies, she could, on a rare lazy day, still make it without having to walk. It was one of her favorite things about living in downtown Sacramento.

As she perused the market amongst throngs of other people, she thought of her ex.

She met Elliot at her coworker's housewarming party just six months after she had returned from teaching in China for two years. Since, at the time, she and Gianna were still rebuilding their friendship, she didn't have many friends and therefore didn't pass up on opportunities to meet new people.

She hadn't noticed Elliot. It was her coworker that

had pointed him out when she noticed that he kept staring at London. She hadn't thought anything of it at first, assuming he was just curious about the solo black woman in a room full of Asian people who also happened to speak fluent Chinese.

She was used to that kind of stare. But his had been different somehow, she realized, after stealing an occasional glance from across the room.

They had eventually ended up in the kitchen at the same time, and she introduced herself to him. He looked at her, his eyes dark and intense behind square shaped glasses, his black hair teasing the top of his left eyebrow, before he responded.

They had talked for a few minutes before going their separate ways again. As the night wore on, she caught him watching her a few times and decided to do something about it. So she asked for his number.

When he finally agreed to go on a date, she saw an entirely different side of him. No longer reserved and hampered by whatever had held him back at the party, he came alive whenever they were together.

And they couldn't keep their hands off of each other. For weeks they spent more time in her studio apartment than they did out in public.

Then, about two months later, it dawned on her that they never really went out on dates. Oh, they would go to the movies on occasion, but if she wanted to go out to dinner, he always had some excuse for why he couldn't.

When she brought it up, he had been brutally honest, which she both loathed and appreciated.

He hadn't wanted his family or friends to find out about their relationship. His parents, he shared, were afraid of black people because of the Los Angeles Riots in 1992.

In his opinion, they had every right to be afraid of black people because Korean businesses had been targeted during that period of civil and racial unrest. He understood and respected their fear, even if it meant that they would never allow him to be with a black woman. He was only interested in marrying a Korean woman, but he liked messing around with other women.

London had experienced a wide plethora of bigotry, racism, stereotyping, and other micro aggressions because of her ethnicity, but that moment had certainly been a first.

That he could so easily accept and dismiss his parents prejudice was hurtful enough. But bringing her into it, fully knowing it would only ever be nothing more than sex while she remained unaware?

She had felt so used.

She didn't begrudge Elliot because she understood that family could and often was an important driving force in determining many aspects of one's life. Her own family struggled to understand nearly every decision she had made.

When she had chosen to attend the University of California, Los Angeles to double major in Linguistics and Asian Languages and Cultures, and Linguistics and Spanish, her parents hadn't hidden their disappointment.

Why would she choose to study other people's language and cultures instead of attending a historically black college where she could study her own, they had wondered.

She had responded by asking them why she was expected to do what they had not. They lived their own lives, hadn't they, regardless of whatever expectations came with the color of their skin. She didn't think it was fair for her to be expected to lead or live her life a certain way just because she was black.

That conversation had helped her parents come around a bit, and with time, they embraced the work that she had done teaching English in China and working at Disability Rights California.

They let her live her life, and defended her choices to the handful of extended family that sometimes looked at her like she was from another planet.

She knew that not everyone's family respected each other's individual choices. So no, she couldn't begrudge Elliot's situation. But she couldn't forgive him for using her.

And she learned a valuable lesson. Never chase after a man, especially an Asian one.

∞∞∞∞∞∞∞

She should have known that she would run into Elliot later that week. It had been a while since she had recalled what had happened between them. It just somehow made twisted sense that thinking of him that much would make their paths cross.

Of course, the fact that he worked at the Public Employment Relations Board, which was located a few blocks from her office, didn't help either. She typically ran into him once or twice a month. Sometimes they passed each other walking on the street. Other times, like now, they hit up the coffee shop at the same time.

London watched him while he ordered. He wore navy slacks and a gray dress shirt. Neither fit perfectly and were just slightly baggy on his thin frame. It was typical of him, she realized now. He never put as much effort into his work attire as he did his off the clock attire. He was still attractive. Yet, she found herself wondering what exactly about him had drawn her in.

She hadn't been drawn to him like she had been with Tony. With Tony, her immediate attraction to him had hit her like a brick. The perfect cut of his suit. The hair. The masculine voice. The image of him was so vibrant in her mind that she could picture him standing next to Elliot.

He was a bit taller than Elliot, and she preferred dating taller men. Tony had seemed more confident, even when she made him fumble. Elliot had acted like she was from another planet at first.

Elliot finished placing his order and walked through the image of Tony that she had projected beside him. When the image went away, she was startled by the immediate and deep disappointment that she felt. And then she was annoyed.

Shit. She was thinking of him even when she told herself she couldn't and wouldn't go there. Worse, she was comparing him to her ex. What the hell was wrong with her?

She turned her attention to her friend, Iris, who hadn't noticed Elliot yet. She was busy typing on her phone, her black hair curtaining around her face and blocking her view.

She had first met Iris Li when they volunteered at an event hosted by DRC. They had formed a loose, casual relationship after that, keeping in contact primarily through social media. Then, a few years later, they were both hired on at DRC. It was that previous connection that had helped them build their friendship so quickly and seamlessly.

And it was that connection that had eventually led her to the man on the other side of the coffee shop.

Iris finally looked up, letting her cellphone hang from the cross body straps it was attached to. Her hazel eyes swept across the room and stopped on the menu. Then swept back to Elliot.

"Look," Iris said, nudging London and nodding in Elliot's direction.

"Yeah, I saw him," she said, grateful for the interruption into her thoughts about Tony. "It's been a while."

Iris rolled her eyes. "Not long enough."

London chuckled, earning Elliot's attention. He lifted a hand in greeting before standing to the side to wait for his order.

"He's going to talk to us."

"Yep," London agreed.

She tried not to complain, or talk about, this inconvenient part of her life. Elliot, whether she liked it or not, was going to be in and out of her life for the foreseeable future.

Elliot was a friend of Iris' boyfriend, Evan. Not best friend, but close enough that they were both invited to the same birthday or dinner parties. Or house warming parties, she thought dryly, thinking of the night that they had met. She wouldn't have to worry about being in Iris and Evan's wedding party with him, should the two ever decide to wed, but he would probably be at the engagement party.

Even though she had broken up with Elliot almost two years ago, he still played a small, recurring role in her life. Still, she probably wouldn't find herself in the situation she was in with Tony.

She hadn't shared that information with Gianna.

The poor thing already threatened to shit bricks every time she mentioned Elliot, so it was something she kept to herself.

Besides, it hadn't been difficult to maintain the illusion of friendliness with Elliot. London was naturally a private person, and as a result, the only people who knew about her and Elliot were her three girl friends. She had assumed that Elliot was equally as private and therefore hadn't told anyone about their relationship.

Even though she had been completely wrong about him, the outcome had made it easier for them to pretend they didn't know each other as intimately as they actually had.

So it didn't bother her that he hung around, waiting for them to finish ordering so he could speak. It was all part of the charade.

"Hey, Iris. London," he called, his attention focusing on London. "How's it going?"

London offered him a small smile. "Can't complain. How are you?"

Elliot shrugged. "I'm alright. I've got a lot going on."

"Evan mentioned that your dad has been having some health issues," Iris shared.

"I'm so sorry," London said, completely sincere. "I hope it's not too serious."

"He's doing better now, thanks," he said, smiling weakly. "It's just put some things into different perspectives."

"I can imagine. I hope everything works out."

"Yeah, me too. Listen, do you think we could—"

"There's our drinks!" Iris interrupted. "We should go or we'll be late for our meeting, London. I'm glad you're dad is doing well. See you around!"

London barely had time to blink before Iris tugged her toward the counter to grab their drinks. Once in hand, Iris moved quickly to the door. London said nothing and followed Iris until she slowed her pace a block away.

"So why did you need to make up a meeting that we don't have to get away from Elliot?" London asked.

"He was going to ask you out!" Iris hissed.

She blinked in surprise, and then laughed. "I doubt it."

"He recently broke up with his girlfriend."

"And? Do you really think he would think I would agree to be his rebound?"

"We're talking about a man, aren't we?"

London shrugged. "Touché."

"All of that different perspective crap. Wouldn't be surprised if he's looking to get back with the best thing he's ever had."

"First off, thank you. I am the best. Second, I need to see an exorcist or psychic or something. There has to be a way to get rid of whatever it is about me that attracts the worst men."

"Well, why don't I help you with the research?"

Iris laughed, and then pulled her into their building to do just that.

CHAPTER 3

Game day at the Golden 1 Center wasn't always hectic. As the Marketing Account Manager for the Sacramento Kings, Tony managed a small team of five that handled the day-to-day responsibilities of business development, such as working with sales and marketing teams to prepare presentations or designing marketing strategies and media proposals.

It was only on days like this, when one of their corporate partners was in the building, that he felt the stress of his position. And when that partner was representing the Golden 1 Credit Union, Sacramento's homegrown bank and where the arena's name originated, the pressure was on.

He trusted his staff and all the employees at Golden 1, but Frank Finely required, and expected, Tony's personal time and attention.

Frank was hosting several employees from Disability Rights California, a non-profit organization that protects and advocates for the rights of people with disabilities.

Tony had steered Frank, who he suspected was just looking for a tax write off, toward this organization because of the work they did. He looked at it as a win for both, while Frank liked being able to come off as the generous benefactor.

Receiving free tickets to an NBA game would have sufficed, but Frank wanted to see and be seen, so he had opened up his wallet, and his suite.

Frank would expect the provided meals and service to be a positive reflection of his status, and it was Tony's job to deliver. So, instead of heading home after a day of back-to-back meetings, he was overseeing every stage of the preparations.

Tony took stock of the suite. A large flat screen TV hung tidily against a wall of taupe glass subway tiles. Beneath the screen, warming trays and platters of food were arranged meticulously.

The golden brown cabinets held extra plates, server ware, and napkins. A refrigerator paneled in the same golden brown held an assortment of beverages. A rectangular island provided bar seating for four on each side.

The opposite wall featured yet another large screen TV, and guests could enjoy this screen while lounging on a purple leather couch. Since he was a true Kings fan, he preferred the two rows of stadium style seating where guests could sit in one of ten plush, leather seats and watch the actual game and all that went with it.

Finally satisfied that everything was in order an hour before the game, Tony glanced at his watch. He headed to his office, and had just enough time to grab his suit jacket and refresh his deodorant and cologne before he received a text from one of the suite managers that guests were starting to arrive. Since he wanted to be near by when Frank arrived, Tony hung out in the empty suite next door.

While he waited, he took out his phone and found a few annoyed text messages from Oliver. Apparently Gianna never responded to any of Oliver's text messages, and though it had been two weeks since he had met her, Oliver was still blaming him.

Tony argued that she might not have found him as interesting as he seemed to think he was, but Oliver kept insisting that it was his fault.

Tony knew Oliver didn't care that he had struck out with Gianna, whatever the reason. He just wanted to give Tony hell for fucking up with London.

As if he wasn't doing that all on his own. He felt just a little bit more miserable each passing day, knowing that it was bringing him closer to Jun's wedding when he would see her again.

He was dreading it. He was anxiously anticipating it. If that rollercoaster of mixed emotions didn't equate to a living hell, he wasn't sure what would.

He finally received notification that Frank was in the suite so he made his away over. When he entered, there were a handful of people mingling about, helping themselves to food or admiring the view of the court from this high up.

Frank, wearing a crisp blue suit, was among the latter group. He was making his way toward him, his eyes on Frank, when the person next to Frank laughed.

The sound was soft and full of mirth, and familiar enough to make his heart skip a beat. He followed Frank's eyes, which were trained on the woman next to him, and cursed his luck yet again.

Because there she was. The woman he wanted, and couldn't have, flirting with a man who could. He was instantly jealous, and struggled to keep it off his face when Frank finally saw him.

"Tony, there you are! London, you've got to meet Tony. He takes care of everything here for me." He leaned closer to her, dropping the volume of his voice.

"I'm sure he'd set you up too, if I asked him to."

Frank placed his hand on the small of London's back, guiding her forward. Tony felt his jealousy ramp up when Frank didn't remove his hand, letting it linger there instead as if the thought of not touching her was unbearable.

London, wearing a purple t-shirt with the Sac Kings logo displayed prominently on the front, looked at him and sent him another one of those forced smiles as they stopped in front of him, her eyes flicking over him in dismissal.

"Nice to meet you," she said coolly, not bothering to offer her hand. She turned to Frank. "I'm going to grab something to eat."

Frank held his hand out to Tony, but he watched London walk away with a lecherous look on his face that made Tony grind his teeth.

He knew Frank was twelve years his senior, and assumed London was much closer to his age than the man that was currently staring at her ass.

Not that their age difference mattered to Frank, who believed that all his money made up for any age differences. Well, he would be damned if he let him get his hooks in London.

Tony gripped Frank's hand tighter than necessary, drawing the man's attention away from London.

"It's a pleasure having you back, Frank. How have you been?"

Frank grinned. "Great. Absolutely great. Hey, where's the champagne?"

Tony worked to keep his voice even. "It wasn't on your list of requests—I personally checked off every item before you got here, but I can have some brought in."

"Yeah, you do that," he said, searching the room for London.

"Okay. I'll email the additional invoice to your secretary."

Frank's lips pressed together, forming a thin line. Tony walked away before he could say anything, knowing he had disappointed him by not giving him the champagne for free.

But there was no way he would do that knowing that Frank hoped to make his quarry more amenable with alcohol. Disgusted, he relayed the information to the server, who used the room's tablet to place the order.

This was the part of his job that he hated. He wanted nothing more than to put Frank in his place, but his position dictated that he keep the man happy.

Well, this time, he was going to tow the line a little by hanging around longer than he normally would. So he chatted up a few of the guests who had obviously only come here for the experience and not the actual basketball game.

The true basketball fans took advantage of the theatre-sized seats to watch the game. London had finally made her way over there after flirting with Frank for a few minutes when he insisted on getting her a glass of champagne.

How could she flirt with that pile of sleaze, but pretend, yet again, that she had never met him before? He had been nothing but a perfect gentleman, except minus the part where he hadn't asked for her number even though it had been clear that he was interested in her.

Meanwhile, she ignored Tony, but didn't seem to mind how thick Frank was laying it on. And he kept touching her arm or her hand as if he had every right to. He wanted to rip the man's hands off and shove them down his throat.

Fortunately for his growing temper, but unfortunately for Frank, London sat between two others to watch the game, forcing Frank to sit behind her. He relaxed a little bit and hung back next to the door, ready to protect her from Frank, and herself, if needed.

At halftime, London rose from her seat. As soon as she turned, she saw him. It was bad enough that she had to deal with Forward Frank. Having Tony there, who had conveniently left out that he worked for the Sacramento Kings when they had talked about the team, only added to her annoyance.

And instead of feeling nothing but righteous fury, she couldn't help but notice how good he had looked. Standing there in a bespoke light gray suit, his eyes watching her, looking hotter than the law should allow. She didn't want to feel that hum of attraction to him.

London hooked her arm through Iris' as they moved toward the buffet.

"Help me," she whispered.

Iris bit the inside of her cheek. "You mean you're not interested in old white dudes?"

They broke apart to pick up plates. London looked up briefly and saw that Frank was talking to Tony. Grateful for the reprieve, she relaxed a little.

"Not even a little bit."

Iris chuckled. "Let's fill up here, mingle for bit, and then go to the bar. Evan was able to score some nose bleeds, but said he'll be at the bar most of the night."

"Sounds good. How's the house hunt going?""

Iris groaned. "Shitty. Makes me think we're insane

for trying to buy a house together before we're even engaged."

"It's absolutely insane," she agreed, pausing a moment to eat. "But it's also so you and Evan that not buying the house first makes less sense."

"Ugh, that's what my cousin said."

"What's the problem?"

"We can't seem to agree on anything. I hate it, but he loves it. I love it, and he hates it. And when we do agree, even reluctantly, somebody comes in and swoops it up before we can finalize our offer. It's exhausting."

"That sounds exhausting. I wish I could help make it easier for you."

"Same. But the realtor you told us about has been great, so there's that." She leaned forward a bit. "The old guy is on his way over here."

"Shit. Distract him. I'll go to the bathroom and then meet you at the bar."

She handed Iris her plate and made a beeline for the door, pretending she didn't hear Frank when he called her name. But her luck stopped there. Tony held the door open and stepped out into the hall with her.

"Can I talk to you for a minute?"

"I'm sorry, sir," she said, her voice all sweet and sour. "I'm not interested in whatever you're selling."

Tony stopped in surprise. "Why are you pretending you don't know me?"

"I don't know you," she responded, searching for signs for the bathroom where she could escape.

"The guy you were flirting with the other day," he said, his voice full of annoyance. "The same way you were flirting with that sleaze bag."

Now she looked at him, and she didn't bother to

hide her own annoyance. "Wow. You have no idea what flirting is, do you? You're dumber than I thought."

He grabbed her arm. For one insane moment, her heart raced in anticipation. The determined and heated look on his face spoke of a man who went after what he wanted, and she believed for one false moment that she was it.

She let him lead her into the empty suite next door, too caught up in what she foolishly hoped would come next to stop him. Finally, she thought irrationally, and cursed her traitorous emotions.

The heat of his hand on her arm and the scent of his cologne further clouded her judgment, and she had to check the urge to throw herself into his arms when she heard the door close behind him. But he let her go before he rounded on her.

"What the hell is your problem?"

The bite in his voice brought her back to reality, and her eyes snapped up from gazing at his lips to meet his.

"I don't have one, but you will if you ever put your hands on me like that again."

"Look, I'm just trying to figure out what's going on here."

"There's nothing to figure out, and there's nothing going on here," she said, standing taller and jutting her chin out stubbornly.

"That's bullshit," he protested.

He wanted to shake her. He wanted to grab her and never let go. Couldn't she see how crazy she was making him?

"Agree to disagree," she said with a careless shrug.

He wiped his hands over his face. "Are you always this infuriating?"

"No. Are you?"

"What the hell did I do to you?" He demanded, stepping forward to close the gap between them.

"Nothing, you idiot," she said, trying to sidestep around him. He kept blocking her. "Just wasted my time. Then, and now."

"What the hell does that mean?"

London closed her eyes for a brief second, praying for patience, but glad that she was coming back to her senses.

"You really are stupid. Get out of my way."

"No. Damn it," he sighed. "I haven't been able to stop thinking about you since we met. Will you just talk to me?"

She took a deep breath, refusing to be swayed by his confession. She looked over his shoulder.

"I'm not interested. I don't know how I can be more clear."

"Fine," he said quietly.

"Fine," she whispered, waiting for him to move.

He didn't. He just stood there, watching her, as the game started back up behind her. She caved to the tense silence before he did and eventually her eyes met his.

He saw something, like a softening plea, before she rolled her shoulders and her eyes hardened. Then she stepped around him, stirring the air with her scent.

He closed his eyes, breathing her in. When the door didn't open right away, he knew she was hesitating. Knew she was giving him one more chance.

Knew she must want him as much as he wanted her.

Tony turned his head, saw her in the corner of his eye as she opened the door.

"This isn't over."

She slipped out and the door clicked quietly shut behind her.

Alone, he took a deep breath, fighting every instinct to go after her. He was too riled up, and he had already made such a humongous mess of this entire thing. He needed to wait for calm before he approached her again.

He hadn't imagined the pull of their attraction each time their eyes met, then and now. And even though he had given her no reason to trust him, there was something between them. He wanted her, and only wanted her more now that he had seen her again.

He wasn't about to walk away from something he wanted. Not this time. He was tired of living his life that way.

He was going to make London his, no matter the consequences.

CHAPTER 4

Tony paced his office, his nerves a complete jumble. He glanced at the clock and saw that it was fifteen minutes shy of noon. Phase one of his plan was already in motion so he wasn't sure why he was obsessing over the lunch hour actually starting at noon.

After a near sleepless night, he decided he needed to find ways to insert himself into London's life to soften her hard stance against him before the wedding in four weeks. If he could somehow convince her that he wanted to repent for mishandling things, then she might be open to actually speaking to him.

Phase one was a catered lunch for DRC from local restaurant, South. South was a homegrown restaurant cooking up some of the most delicious Southern cuisine he had ever tasted. It was a rare day when a line hadn't formed outside the doors thirty minutes to an hour before the restaurant opened its doors.

He had begged and pleaded and left a substantial tip to get them to agree to cater a lunch for DRC with such short notice, and luckily they had agreed. After lunch was confirmed, he sent an email to DRC's director offering up a free meal to thank his staff for all they did for people with disabilities.

Tony had drafted the email as if it was from him on

behalf of the Sac Kings. He hoped that the staff would know that it had come from him. Not that he was looking for accolades or thanks.

He wanted London to think of him and know that he was really doing it for her.

The only connection he could use at this point was her job, and he knew he was pushing the boundaries there. Since he didn't want to come off like he was stalking her at her place of work, he catered for the entire group.

Phase two and three would mean pushing even harder against that boundary, and maybe even crossing a line. But it was the only feasible way to rebuild the bridge to her.

He had briefly considered reaching out to Jun, but dismissed that idea almost immediately. Jun hadn't called him out for what happened with London at Ella's so that meant he didn't know. He wanted to keep it that way.

He wasn't ready to explain why he needed help to get on London's good side. Furthermore, he didn't want to create any drama for his friend on his wedding and honeymoon. The less Jun knew, the better.

He had to use what little resources he had in a relatively short time frame.

He didn't know what he would do about his parents if he managed to get her to go out with him. He couldn't even think about it yet.

He did think about all the women he had been attracted to or interested in since he was a teenager. Sacramento was a very diverse city with pockets of cultural or ethnic communities. He knew that it was because of that exposure that he had always been inclined toward interracial dating.

He didn't know when or why his attraction to African American women began to take precedence, but he did know it had become increasingly difficult to ignore. And even harder to settle for something other than what he really wanted.

Someday, he would have to reconcile what he wanted for his own life with the life his parents wanted for him.

It might be out of order, but the first step in his mind was getting the girl.

Tony took a deep breath and looked at the clock. It was noon. Hopefully London was serving herself a plate of delicious food and wondering if he was doing this for her.

And wondering what he would do next.

∞∞∞∞∞∞∞∞

At eight am, news of a catered lunch for DRC employees spread through the building like wildfire. It was rare for DRC to be treated so handsomely back to back. The game tickets were enough to keep them feeling like other's valued their work as much as they did for at least a year. Following that up with a free meal was the ultimate cherry on top. It made for one exciting Friday.

By nine am, a group had formed to prepare the conference room for the impromptu lunch. Over the next hour, they moved tables and chairs. Someone even ran out to the store for a tablecloth for the table they had designated for the food.

While they set up and gathered supplies, London overheard several conversations about Tony. Many of her coworkers had had an opportunity to speak to him at the game last night and were eager to share their impressions of him. She had to check the urge to grind her teeth every time she heard his name.

She took a break at eleven and headed to the coffee shop. She was tired and a headache was starting to form because she had to work so hard to pretend that she was in just as good of a mood as everyone else.

A part of her was regretting not telling her friends about her encounter with Tony last night. She didn't want them making a big deal out of it like they had the night at Ella's. As long as they kept talking about him, the drama, or whatever it was between them, became that much more important than it actually was. She wanted to put it behind her.

Unfortunately, her own mental and emotional state wasn't cooperating. That's where the regret came in. Perhaps if she had talked to them about it, she wouldn't have been up more than half the night, tossing and turning in bed, recreating the conversation over and over.

She wasn't exactly pleased that so many of those recreations had ended up with them naked on the floor.

She wanted to forget him, and it didn't look like he was going to let her off that easy. It annoyed her. If he had shown this much effort from the beginning, things would be completely different.

But she didn't trust him now, and this certainly wasn't helping. She knew what this meal was. Who it was for and what it meant. Tony was trying to make up for being a complete and utter moron. He thought buying lunch for her coworkers would soften her up or somehow make him trustworthy.

As she stepped inside the coffee shop, London

thought about not eating out of pure spite. She had packed a lunch after all. He wouldn't know, but she would. It would probably make her feel better.

"Hey, London."

She felt the usual tick of annoyance that she always felt whenever she and Elliot crossed paths. Only this time, given her current mood, it felt a bit more pronounced than usual. She couldn't stop the frustrated sigh from escaping.

Elliot lifted an eyebrow. "Bad day?"

"Yeah, a little bit," she said, hoping to warn him off.

"That sucks. Can I get your drink? Maybe that will help. Vanilla latte right?"

She paused, not expecting him to respond that way, let alone remember her favorite drink. He watched her, his eyes sincere. She didn't have the heart to be cruel just because she was in a bad mood, so she nodded her head in consent.

After he placed their order, they moved off to the side to wait. She expected him to say something, but he just stood there silently, his hands tucked into the pockets of his jeans. Grateful, she enjoyed the momentary peace and watched the crowd while they waited.

He retrieved their order when it came up, then held the door open for her.

"Can I walk you back? There's something I've been wanting to ask you."

There it was, she thought, and sighed. "Okay."

"I know this isn't the best time. I wish I could wait but it's just that I've been thinking about this for a while and I know if I don't say something then I'll make myself crazier or you'll end up with someone who isn't an idiot like me so I just have to say it. I want you back."

"Um…what?" She stopped a second, too stunned to respond any other way.

"My dad had a bad heart attack. There's not a day of his recovery that he isn't regretting something he's done or didn't do. I don't want that to be me someday. I want you back. I've wanted you back since we broke up. Can you just think about it? That's all I'm asking. Don't say anything yet. Think about it first. I'll try to give you space until you're ready to talk."

London stared after him long after he disappeared around the corner. She shook her head, and then sipped some of her coffee. Then she pinched her arm just to be sure she wasn't sleepwalking.

Discovering that she was in fact awake, she wondered how long she should wait before she told him that there was no way in hell that she would get back with him.

She didn't need time to think it through. She had. She had taken herself there many times in the early days after their break up. She had pictured him crawling back to her, his parents expectations be damned, more times than she cared to count.

In the end, she came to the understanding that even if he did decide to choose her over his family, she could never live with knowing that she had come between them.

As she started up the walk to her office, she cursed her luck. How in the hell did she end up in such a ridiculous triangle? What was it about her that attracted men with so much baggage?

Back at her office, London sat at her desk and logged in. The email the director had forwarded from Tony was open on her desktop. Since she wasn't exactly in her right mind, she briefly considered sending him an email to let him know that she wasn't falling for his tricks. She wanted to call him out.

Fortunately, the coffee was doing its work and since the email clearly indicated that this meal was for the entire group, she knew she couldn't. She didn't want him to know that she knew what he was up to. She wouldn't give him the satisfaction.

Still, it was going to be hard to focus and get anything accomplished today. The atmosphere still buzzed from all of the excitement, and the food coma that followed would make the rest of the day crawl by.

Deciding that enough was enough, she called her boss and asked to take off at twelve because she wasn't feeling well. Thankful that she got the time off approved, she sent out a few final emails before logging out.

She swung by the conference room, grabbed two of South's delicious homemade biscuits, and tried to put the entire day behind her.

∞∞∞∞∞∞∞

She spent nearly the entire weekend thinking about Tony and what he might do next. She wanted to be ready, she told herself, for this next move. She was positive he would make another move.

He would probably send some flowers or some other cheesy thing to her at the office since that was his only way of reaching out to her.

But Monday came and went with no gifts delivered to her desk. He didn't send flowers or chocolate candies on Tuesday. The handwritten heartfelt confession she had pictured tossing smugly into the garbage didn't come on Wednesday.

When she got home on Thursday, she considered that maybe she had misjudged him. Again. Then she decided it was best to wait until Friday. Maybe he was just trying to do something with an even seven days in between so that he didn't seem so desperate.

But when she went home empty handed on Friday, she accepted that last week's meal hadn't been about her or about them after all.

She wanted to be grateful. She didn't want to be bothered with the drama of whatever hang up had prevented him from pursuing her the first time around. It was better that he accepted that nothing was going to happen between them.

Since she was having a harder time than she would have liked being grateful and accepting the truth herself, she woke up Saturday feeling irritated with herself.

Needing a distraction and a reset, London took a rideshare to her favorite restaurant in South Sacramento. New Sun Restaurant served some of the most amazing Chinese cuisine she had ever tasted. It was the closest thing she could get to the food she had in China. The comfort food and familiarity would surely put her in a better mood.

Mrs. Yu and Mr. Cheng, the restaurants owners, were some of her favorite people. London had first earned a place on Mrs. Yu's good side a few years earlier when London pretended to be her lawyer and threatened to sue an irate and racist customer on her behalf.

She had thrown enough legal jargon around that she had picked up from hanging around DRC's lawyers to give the man pause. She liked to think that hearing her speak to Mrs. Yu in Mandarin fully convinced him to take his shit somewhere else.

Whatever the case, he high tailed it out of there, and the interaction opened the door to a relationship with Mrs. Yu. At first, they only viewed each other as valuable resources. London would share resources or contacts she obtained through her work, which Mrs. Yu then passed on to friends, family, and the community, and Mrs. Yu shared information about resources she learned about from her community.

They came together in their own unique way to help others.

Eventually that relationship became true friendship, and maybe something more, London thought with a small smile as she climbed from the car. On more than one occasion, Mrs. Yu had suggested that London and her son should get together. Unfortunately, their paths hadn't crossed just yet.

Mrs. Yu's husband, Mr. Cheng, was more reserved and often came across as unfriendly. London felt that it was just a tough guy act. He didn't want anyone to know that he was really a sweetheart. Fortunately, she knew just how to soften him up.

Holding the pie box close to her, London entered the restaurant. They had only been open for about a half hour so it wasn't busy just yet. Since she timed it that way, Mrs. Yu greeted and seated her right away.

Mrs. Yu, short and thin, patted her tummy and looked at the box.

"I gain five pounds already just thinking about eating that," she said.

London grinned, feeling the stress melt away after hearing the beauty that was the Mandarin language. Happy to speak the language, she responded in kind.

"I haven't been by in a while so I figured this was well overdue."

Mrs. Yu clucked her tongue. "You need to eat it. You look like you've lost weight. Is that job stressing you out?"

London sighed. "Not the job."

"Ah, a man then. Ditch him. Date my son. Though I'm sure he would be just as much trouble. That boy hasn't been around to help since the New Year. You both work too hard."

"You work too hard too, Mrs. Yu."

She waved her towel in disagreement. "I'll send him out and get them started on your usual."

"Yes, please."

While she waited for Mr. Cheng to come out, London wished she could meet their son. At least she knew that they would be okay with the interracial relationship. But, she wasn't that lucky. She seemed only to attract men who were ultimately unavailable in some way.

Mr. Cheng sauntered over, his round belly already covered in food scraps and drippings. His eyes lit up for the briefest moment before he fixed a stern look on his face. She bit her tongue so she wouldn't grin.

"Your order would be out faster if you didn't interrupt me," he complained, though there was no heat or censor in his voice to indicate that he was upset.

Knowing that this was part of the tough guy role he played with her, she held out the box to him.

"Ah, my apologies, Mr. Cheng. Don't let me keep you. Thank you for the meal."

He opened the box and his eyes lit up again. "Sweet potato?"

"Yes, sir."

"Thank you," he said, giving her a small smile before walking away.

Mrs. Yu came out as he went back in the kitchen, saying something that London couldn't hear. She assumed he was complaining again when Mrs. Yu looked over at her and rolled her eyes.

London grinned in response. He played hard to get, but she was positive that Mr. Cheng liked her as much as Mrs. Yu did.

Content, she sat back and watched people come and go, finally feeling grateful, and accepted what couldn't, and wouldn't be.

∞∞∞∞∞∞∞

London's phone rang, interrupting her train of thought on the report she was writing up. Scowling, she glanced at the caller ID and saw it was the front desk. It was rare, but not uncommon for a client to drop by, and she could only assume that was the reason for the call.

"Hey, what's up?" She answered.

"Certified mail up here for you. He says you have to sign for it."

"Huh. I wasn't expecting anything. I'm on my way."

London slipped back into her heels before pushing away from the desk to stand. She navigated the tight gathering of cubicles, waving to those who looked up as she passed by. It was a quiet Monday, which was typical, with most people working at their desk. Very few client meetings took place on Mondays.

When she stepped into the lobby, she spotted the courier immediately. His neon green polo shirt made him impossible to miss.

"Hi. I'm London," she said, holding up her badge.

"Thanks. Just sign here," he passed her his clipboard and waited. Then he exchanged it for the envelope. "Thanks. Have a great day."

"You too," she said distractedly, wondering what was in the envelope.

She badged back into the office side and broke the envelope's seal as she made her way to her desk. She recognized the top of the Kings logo immediately, and butterflies danced in her stomach in response. Cursing under her breath, she quickly went to her desk and sat.

He was good, she thought, realizing she hadn't given him enough credit. Reluctantly, she admired his tactic and efforts. Because he hadn't made an effort to reach out to her last week, she forced herself to put him out of her mind. She hadn't been prepared for this, and he must have known that she wouldn't be.

Inside was a white envelope with the Kings logo displayed prominently in the left-hand corner. Turning it around, she lifted the flap and sucked in a breath. Tickets. There were four tickets to Thursday's game, and they were amazing seats, she realized after looking closer.

He also included his business card. She brushed her fingers over his name before she could stop herself. On the back of his card, she found a note written in his neat handwriting.

London,

I'm sorry for my horrible behavior at the game two weeks ago. I have no excuses. Please accept these tickets for Thursday's game to make up for interfering with what should have been an enjoyable and stress free night.

—Tony

London slipped the card and tickets back in the envelope and leaned back in her chair. Tapping the envelope against her hand, she considered what she should do. Despite her best efforts, she had spent all of last week thinking about him, and nearly the entire weekend. Just when she was prepared to fully put him out of her mind, he sprung up again with a completely unexpected move.

Even if the tickets had cost him nothing, which she believed was a strong possibility, he was wise enough to assume that his apology would mean a lot more to her than if he had sent flowers instead.

She didn't believe, not for a second, that these tickets were meant to be just an apology. He was courting her in his own unique and unpredictable way. She really couldn't think of a better word for it than that. If she accepted them, she might give him the impression that she was cosigning his pursuit, and that just wasn't the case.

But only an idiot would turn down free tickets to watch their favorite team play.

He was good, she thought again. Wanting to be better, she sat up and unlocked her computer. After pulling up her email, she scrolled through her trash to find the email the director had forwarded to the team with Tony's email on it. Locating it, she started a new email.

To: Tony Cheng

From: London Henderson

Subject: Kings Tickets

I appreciate the apology, and the tickets.

Before I can accept them, I need your word that you'll keep your distance. I also want to make sure that you understand that accepting these tickets doesn't mean that I've changed my opinion about you.

If we're clear on that, I'll be there. If not, I'll find someone else to give them to.

London

She read over her words a few times, trying to decide if she wanted to change or add anything more. She was over thinking it, which is probably exactly what he wanted. Annoyed, she copied his address into her email and hit send.

Five minutes later, her computer chimed, signaling the arrival of a new email. She had barely started working on her report. She bit her lip, wondering if it was from him, and quickly realized he had messed her up again. She was going to spend the rest of the day too distracted to work because she was waiting on his response.

London scowled at her computer, incredibly annoyed. Worse, she couldn't complain to her friends because she still hadn't told them about running into

Tony at the game. She definitely couldn't say anything now. They would make a big deal about it or try to pressure her into giving him the second chance that he so obviously wanted.

It was bad enough that she was starting to second-guess herself. She didn't need her friend's in her ear as well.

As much as she wanted to deny it, she was a little flattered by his not exactly subtle effort to win her affections. And when she thought of how hot he looked in those suits? Yeah, she definitely needed to keep her distance or risk doing something incredibly stupid.

She muted her computer and ignored all emails until noon. It was more difficult than she cared to admit. When she finally checked her inbox, her heart raced when she saw his name.

To: London Henderson

From: Tony Cheng

Subject: Re: Kings Tickets

London,

You have every right to be suspicious. I promise that I will not bother you, and while I hate to admit it, I know that you don't trust me yet.

I'm sorry. For everything. Please enjoy the game.

Tony

It made her scowl again. It was so understanding, and so perfectly written that it was almost cliché. And yet she couldn't stop her damn heart from thawing a little of the ice that the logical side of her brain had built around it.

London glanced at her calendar as she stood. She had three weeks to make sure the ice was rock solid. If she allowed him to melt her defenses when they had to travel together for the wedding…

She let the thought hang, not wanting to finish it, and reminded her heart that she couldn't trust him with it.

∞∞∞∞∞∞∞

Tony listened with half an ear while the camera and sound techs talked and joked about the bets they had placed on tonight's game. He pretended to be engaged in their conversation, but his thoughts were far from the upcoming game.

The arena was filling, though not quickly. Most people didn't care to be present for all of the opening commentary or the singing of the national anthem. Others mingled at the Sierra Nevada Draught House. Named for the Sierra Nevada Brewing Company, which was founded in Chico, California, the bar provided an opportunity to take in some of the best views of the arena bowl.

If she wasn't up there, she had several other options just a stone throw away from the arena's entrance. Downtown Commons, or DOCO for short, had been transformed into the ultimate social scene with its assortment of restaurants and bars.

He hoped that whomever she brought with her to the game were also true basketball fans that wouldn't want to miss the tip-off.

It suddenly occurred to him that she could bring a date with her. The thought made him just a little bit nauseous. A woman as funny and attractive as London was likely had a man who was just as eager as he was to be with her.

Refusing to entertain that possibility, he tried to tune back into the guys conversation. It was rare for him to hang out in the arena during a game since he was typically up in the suites. Still, no one would question him loitering around even if he wasn't paying attention to them.

He wanted to see her. Needed to see her. It would give him just a little bit of hope that he could change her mind.

He couldn't build this bridge by using clichés, and he couldn't let her know, not yet, that he still planned to pursue her. He hoped that these gestures would convince her that he wasn't as terrible as he made himself out to be.

The hit his finances took when he purchased those tickets was a great reminder that he couldn't afford to keep fucking up with her. His employee discount only went so far.

He had chosen those seats carefully. Five rows up from courtside and within direct few of the tech and camera box. He could see her from this spot. If she showed up, he would take it as a sign that his plan was working.

Yes, he had promised not to bother her, but since she didn't put any other constraints on that request, he took that to mean that it only applied to tonight. He had to earn her trust so he could have another chance.

So he watched for her. By the time she finally arrived, his heart had jumped in false anticipation so many times that the actual sight of her left him feeling just a little bit dizzy.

She wasn't dressed like a fan this time. As his eyes passed briefly over Valerie, Gianna, and the woman he had seen her talking to in the suite, he saw that they were dressed for a girl's night out.

Her make up was sultry and mysterious. She wore a long sleeved gold satin blouse that tied at the side and paired it with black form fitting pants. He cursed every man who was sitting behind her and wished he were closer.

He stared. He couldn't help it. The need for her filled him up and overflowed. When she looked over, her eyes scanning the crowd as if she sensed his eyes on her, his heart raced. When their eyes met and locked, it stopped.

He tilted his head calmly, casually, though he felt anything but, and then turned to walk away. He promised not to bother her, and he would honor it by not staring at her all night.

It was enough that she was there. Believing his plan was working, he went home to finalize the details for phase three.

CHAPTER 5

"Hey, girl. Want to go for a coffee run?"

London looked up from her computer screen to see Iris leaning against her cubicle. She wore a sunny floral print dress that made her want to venture outdoors, but she had her reasons for sticking close to the office these days.

"Can you bring me something back?"

"Why can't you go with me? What are you working on?"

She stepped forward to peer at London's dual monitors and saw email on one and Amazon on the other.

"I'm very busy," London explained with a grin.

"I can see that. Come on. Let's go get some sun."

London glanced at the clock. It was just shy of ten am, which meant many other people would be venturing out for a midmorning coffee run.

"I can go in forty five."

Iris narrowed her eyes. "Oh my god. Are you still avoiding Elliot?"

"Guilty," she confessed without shame.

It had been three weeks since Elliot asked her to consider getting back together. She had no intention of entertaining that insane idea and didn't relish having that conversation with him either. So she tried to avoid the places where she typically ran into him, and any coffee shops in the area were the number one places on the list that she couldn't go to.

"You have got to put that guy out of his misery."

"Nope. He got himself into his misery all on his own. I have every confidence that he can get himself out."

Iris grinned. "When you're right, you're right. But how long are you planning to keep this up? He's going to find a way to bump into you at some point."

"As long as I can. I'm hoping he'll take my silence as a hint to move on."

"He won't."

London scowled. "I know that you're right and it just pisses me off."

Iris shook her head. "Text me your order."

"Thank you!"

A few minutes after Iris left, her office phone rang and the readout said it was from the front desk. She immediately thought of Tony, and a warm feeling settled in her stomach. They were leaving for Hawaii in eight days and she hadn't heard or received anything from him since the game. If he was going to make a move again, it would be soon, unless he was saving it for Hawaii.

"Hey Chris," she answered.

"Package for you," he said.

"I'll be right up," she said and then hung up.

In the lobby, Chris grinned over at Tony. "She's on her way."

Tony let out a small breath. "Thanks for that."

"Who am I to spoil such an attractive surprise," he said, his smile widening.

"Thanks," he replied, not knowing what else to say.

Tony watched the door anxiously while he waited. He knew he was pushing his luck here, but he hoped that ultimately the bold move worked in his favor.

The door swung open, and there she was. She wore a full midi skirt that was pale yellow and a blue and white-checkered quarter sleeve button down shirt. She skidded to a halt in blue heels when their eyes met, her jaw dropping open in surprise.

Recovering quickly, she glanced nervously at Chris before crossing the room to take Tony by the arm. He had to check the urge to pull her into his arms and just breathe her in. He was so focused on how amazing she looked and smelled that he didn't even realize that she was leading him outside until the heat hit him.

"What are you doing here?" She demanded, releasing his arm.

"I brought you something," he said, holding up the white gift bag. "I was just planning to drop it off, but the guy said that you were inside and if I wanted this to get to you and not eaten by someone else, then I should give it to you directly."

She looked at the bag and her heart melted. "Is that Ginger Elizabeth?"

"Yes." She eyed him cautiously, but accepted the bag when he held it out to her. "I wasn't sure what you liked so I went with the twelve piece box of chocolates. I'm sure I've interrupted your day so I'll let you go."

She opened the bag with a wistful sigh. "Why are you doing this?"

He shrugged, watching her closely. "I guess I've decided to take my own advice. You look absolutely stunning, London. It's a pleasure seeing you again. Until next week."

London stared after him as he walked away, wondering what he meant. Then she remembered the first night that they met when he told her that she should always go after what she wanted.

He was definitely after her, and so far, her defenses weren't holding up as well as she would have liked.

Ginger Elizabeth Chocolates was a chocolate boutique unique to Northern California. Ginger grew up just an hour from Sacramento, and after traveling the country and mastering her craft, she returned to her home state where she opened up several successful shops.

How could Tony have known that Ginger Elizabeth Chocolates was a particular and devastating weakness of hers?

She walked into her office, her nose buried in the bag. She ignored Chris' attempt to engage her, knowing he was the office gossip queen, as she badged in. She decided to forgive him since most people in her office also loved Ginger Elizabeth's and probably would have tried to eat the chocolate before it got to her.

She set the bag on her desk and saw the note lying inside.

London,

I know I don't deserve it, but I hope you'll give me the opportunity to explain what happened that night we met. I can't wait to see you again.

—Tony

London collapsed in her chair. Over the last three weeks, she had only managed to keep Tony off her mind for brief snippets at a time. She found herself feeling a range of emotion: suspicion, wariness, and distrust. Attraction, interest, curiosity, lust—god he had looked so good today in that suit.

He didn't deserve a second chance. She didn't want to hear his excuses. Even as the thought formed, she knew it to be a lie. She wanted to know, and god help her, she wanted to give him a second chance even though every instinct warned her not to.

She popped a piece of chocolate in her mouth, nearly moaned when it melted against her tongue, and wondered what the hell she was going to do.

∞∞∞∞∞∞∞∞

London had initially been intrigued, happy even, when Valerie had requested that as many guests as possible have the same travel itinerary to their destination wedding.

It made the union of their two lives more than just a symbolic event. Here were two people, who had separate families and friends and lives, that acknowledged that those things would also be joined when they wed, and strived to create as many scenarios as possible to bring the two together seamlessly.

But that was how she felt then. She absolutely hated the idea now.

London tried desperately to focus her attention solely on the movie she watched on her tablet. She had been ignoring Tony since they had arrived bright and early at the airport that morning, but unfortunately, it did not stop him from somehow always managing to be near her or in her space.

When she purposefully chose the longer security line, he did the same. Using the restrooms at the opposite side of the terminal? Same. He tried to cover up the obvious fact that he was waiting for her to come out by taking his sweet time placing his water bottle back in his backpack, but she hadn't been fooled.

She stuck close to Gianna after that, and drew Mika into their conversation as well as an added level of protection. When it came time to board, she found herself annoyed that most of them had ended up in the same boarding group, while everyone else seemed to be ecstatic.

They took advantage of Sacramento Airport's dual boarding option and immediately headed straight to the back of the plane when it was time to board. Tony had been one of the first in their group to get on the plane, but he somehow still managed to secure a seat on her row.

Even from her window seat she could smell the spicy and compelling blend of his cologne, and was slowly going mad. To make matters worse, he looked just as good in linen shorts and a simple navy blue t-shirt as he had wearing the suits she had only ever seen him in.

What the hell was wrong with her? How could she still be so attracted to a man who so obviously had some hang up that had prevented him from asking her out? Now all of the sudden he could go after her?

But maybe whatever had been the issue was no longer an issue.

No, she thought fiercely. *Just no.* She already decided that she wasn't going to go there with him. This back and forth had to stop. Needing a break, and air that didn't smell so provocative, she nudged Gianna so she could go to the restroom.

Gianna turned to glare at Tony the moment London headed down the aisle. She waited until she heard the door close before she spoke.

"Alright, slick. You want to tell me what sort of game you're playing with my friend?"

"No game," he promised, holding up his hands as if that proved his innocence. "None at all, which should explain why I'm on your shit list."

Gianna narrowed her eyes, appreciating that he knew his place. "And what makes you think you deserve to be off of it?"

"Nothing. I didn't think I had a chance then, and I'm not really sure I have one now, but I want to try this time. I've been thinking about her everyday since we met, and after that night at the game—"

"Wait," she held out her hand to stop him, sat up straight. "What night at what game?"

"We bumped into each other at a Kings game last month. The night DRC was invited. I made an ass of myself again so I sent her four tickets to another game."

"You were there that night? And those amazing seats came from you?"

"Uh, yeah, since I work for the Kings…" he trailed off, realizing that the obvious statement only needed to be made for one reason. "She didn't tell you. About any of it. Why not?"

"Don't know exactly, but I might be able to guess. Hmm," she said thoughtfully before moving to the window seat. "Interesting."

Before he could ask her to elaborate, London cleared her throat beside him. He watched her closely as he got up from his seat and stepped into the aisle so she could squeeze back in.

"Hey," she complained to Gianna. "Move."

"I need a nap. You ride bitch now."

London sat and leaned over to whisper angrily. "Gianna. Come on."

"Nuh uh. You can tell me all about what happens next, and," she emphasized with a lift of her eyebrow in Tony's direction. "The night at the Kings game and how you really got those four tickets, when we get to our room."

When London's mouth fell open in shock, Gianna merely put her headphones back on in response before snuggling up against the window with her eyes closed.

Trapped, London scowled and snatched her tablet from the seat back pocket in front of Gianna. She put her headphones on and blasted the audio as high as it would go.

Though she was sure he was purposefully crowding her space by bumping his leg against hers whenever he moved, London refused to acknowledge his presence.

He gave her exactly ten minutes of peace before he leaned toward her and pulled out one of her headphone earpieces.

"So you're really going to ignore me for the next two hours?" He whispered, his breath fanning her ear.

London gritted her teeth, steeling herself against reacting to his closeness.

"This is the first time you've spoken to me."

"I tried talking to you before we boarded."

"Oh," she said, all innocence. "I must not have been paying attention."

Tony sighed. "Look, can we get together later today? To talk."

"No."

"Alright, I deserve that," he admitted. "But I'm not going to give up. I want you. I've wanted you since the first night we met."

London wanted to ask why. *Why didn't you pursue me then?* But the answer didn't matter because it wouldn't change the fact that she didn't trust him.

So she said nothing. She was just about to reach for her earpiece when his hand covered hers, stopping the movement. Enraged by the flood of heat that rushed through her, she whipped her head around to glare at him.

But he was so close, closer than he should have been, as if he knew exactly how she would react. Her sudden movement caused their lips to brush.

"I warned you not to put your hands on me," she whispered, still as a statue.

He released her hand reluctantly, noted that it was trembling slightly. "If you just let me explain—"

"Pass." She turned away.

"I know you felt that."

"Nope."

London put the earpiece back in, trying to tune him out. But of course her traitorous senses refused to stop thinking about their lips touching, or the feel of his warmth, or his scent.

Unable to focus, she stared blankly at the screen, reminding herself that she didn't want to trust him. Couldn't trust him. She knew there was some reason he didn't pursue her, and she was worried that it was the same reason she had ended things with her ex.

She wouldn't go through that again.

Tony decided it was best to let it go for now, not wanting to push her more than he already had today.

And, it seemed, he may have just inadvertently earned a reluctant ally in Gianna.

If he had to come up with a reason as to why London hadn't told Gianna about the night at the game, he would have had to give serious consideration to her insistence that she wasn't interested in him. He would probably have still been in serious denial about it, but he would have at least given it more consideration.

But Gianna seemed genuinely surprised that London had kept that information to herself. Was she hiding it because she was more interested in him than he thought, and didn't want her friend telling her what she didn't want to hear, like, yes, go out with him? If only he could be so lucky.

When the flight attendant came by to take their order, Tony tapped her arm. She glared at him, reminding him that his touch was still unwanted.

He couldn't help but smile in response, growing fonder of her fiery personality. He imagined it would keep things interesting between them.

While he waited for his drink, he leaned back against the seat and watched her movie. She was watching *Star Wars: Episode IV*. In his experience, men were huge Star Wars nerds, so if she was voluntarily watching it, she had to belong to the rare group of female fans. It had been years since he had seen it himself, and he found himself wanting to watch it again, but with the sound on, of course.

Their drinks arrived, and he touched her thigh this time. She reached for her drink, pulling down her tray table at the same time. Then she banged her elbow against the armrest and ended up tossing the drink in his face.

"Oh, gosh. I'm so, so sorry. I'm such a klutz."

Covered in sticky soda, Tony could only laugh, knowing he still had his work cut out for him. What she didn't know though, was that he didn't mind the chase when the reward promised to be so great.

∞∞∞∞∞∞

"So why didn't you tell us all of this before?"

London let out a frustrated sigh as she placed the last of her swimwear in the drawer. She was having serious second thoughts about agreeing to share a room with Gianna.

Since they were single, and best friends, they hadn't seen the point in paying for separate rooms, and decided instead to use the savings to splurge on excursions on the island.

But it annoyed her that Gianna was pushing Tony at her enough to have her considering paying whatever astronomical price the hotel would charge her to book her own room.

The room featured two full sized beds dressed in crisp white sheets that seemed to lead the eyes to the open patio at the far side of the room. The floor to ceiling glass doors let in light and the beautiful horizon where sky met ocean blue.

Two chairs beckoned her to sit and enjoy the sights and smells. She had hoped to open up the bottle of champagne that she had packed and laze about after the long flight. Instead, they were talking about the last thing she wanted to talk about.

"There was no reason to. Nothing. Happened. Why would I tell you about nothing?"

Gianna flopped on the bed furthest from the view.

"Uhm, because it wasn't nothing. He came on to you."

"And didn't act on it. Again," she emphasized, carrying her empty suitcase over to stash away in the large wardrobe.

"Which just makes me want to find out why he didn't ask for your number. It's better than assuming he's like your ex."

London sat on the other bed and faced Gianna. "So you go find out. I don't care."

Gianna merely rolled her eyes. "He looked just as good today as he did in that suit."

"And your point is?"

"You've got the hots for him!"

London laughed. "I never denied that part."

"So find out what's up so you can have him put out the fire that I know is raging in your panties."

Now she rolled her eyes. "I just think that whatever the reason, it probably isn't good. His parents won't allow it, he already has a girlfriend, or I remind him of an ex."

"Or maybe you just intimidate him"

"I disagree. He was relaxed and approachable at the bar, and I'm sure I gave him all the right signals. And the way he came at me on the plane and at the game? No, intimidation isn't it."

"If you'd just given him your number."

"I would have, with any other guy, but there's a reason he didn't want it. His actions said he wasn't interested, so that's what I'm going with."

Gianna got up and sat next to her, placing a hand on her leg. "His actions are saying he's interested now. I'm just saying it wouldn't hurt to find out. You're going to make yourself crazy trying to ignore him for the next week. But if you get an answer, you can move past it, whatever the outcome."

London scowled, exhausted by her persistence. "Fine. Whatever. I'll set up something with him later."

Gianna rose and stepped up to the side table between their beds. Picking up the phone, she pressed zero to get to the front desk.

"Hi there. How are you doing today? Oh, no. The room is absolutely perfect, thank you. I just have something I really hope that you can help me out with. I'm a bridesmaid for the Koboyashi/Hall wedding…yes, that one. Well, I'm trying to get a hold of one of the groomsmen. His name is Tony. We want to plan a little something for the bride and groom. Can you transfer me to his room? Perfect. Thank you so much. I really appreciate it."

Handing the phone to a gaping London, Gianna plopped back down on her bed. Tony picked up after the second ring.

"Hello?"

"My incredibly annoying friend has convinced me to give you an opportunity to explain why you're an idiot. Meet me at the bar downstairs at 9:30."

There was a brief pause. "How about dinner at 7?"

"Nope."

"See you at 9:30."

∞∞∞∞∞∞∞

"You expect me to believe that the reason you didn't ask me for my number, even though you were so convinced that I was flirting with you and therefore must be interested in you, is because you didn't think you had a chance?"

He couldn't deny that it sounded stupid. It was

stupid. Lies often were. But he wasn't ready to face the real reason, especially since he hadn't figured out how to get around it yet, so he couldn't tell her. He gave her a sheepish grin, and hoped for the best.

"Even if I had a chance, I'd mess it up. Like I already have. Haven't I?"

"Oh, absolutely," she agreed, rolling her eyes as she sipped her wine.

He cringed. "You are incredibly smart, confident, and attractive…I let myself believe that I wasn't good enough for you."

London pursed her lips together. "And what convinced you otherwise?"

"I'm not convinced," he confessed, glad that he could be absolutely honest with this at least. "But I want to try to get there."

"Look—"

"I know I was being both a jealous dick and selfish ass, wanting you for myself but not going after you," he interrupted, worried that she would shoot him down. "Let me fix it. Give me your number. Take a trip with me tomorrow. Go out with me for dinner."

She watched him as she drank the rest of her wine, purposefully making him wait. There were enough plea in his voice to let her know that he was being sincere. It annoyed her to know that it weakened her already crumbling defenses.

But Gianna was right. It would be tough to ignore him, and their mutual attraction, and not wonder why. Or what if. She set down her glass and slid off the barstool.

"You can have my number, but my plans for Hawaii do not include going out on dates."

When she held her hand out for his phone, he

quickly dug into his pocket for it, unlocking it before he gave it to her. He asked for the bill while she put her number in his phone.

Relieved, he decided to push his luck. "How about a walk on the beach? It's on the way back to our rooms."

"Fine."

She led the way out of the bar. He smiled as he followed her to the beach. Once on the sand, they took off their shoes and made their way to the shore.

"If you're being purposefully difficult, I should tell you, I find it incredibly hot."

"Masochist," she said with a snort.

He grinned, then bumped against her lightly. "I want to put my hands on you just to see what you'll do."

She felt the fire Gianna spoke of ignite in her panties, and didn't know how to feel about it.

"So now you're bold all of the sudden?"

He shrugged. "I gotta go all in if this is the last chance I'll get to make up for not going after you the first time. Lots of should have or could have scenarios running through my head since we met."

"Like?" *Why had she asked that?*, she thought, panicking a little.

Tony looked over at her. "Like when I should have taken advantage of the fact that I had you alone, and just a little bit willing, in that suite."

She glared at him. "I wasn't willing."

"Then why did you pause at the door before you left?"

"I didn't."

"Yeah, you did. You wanted me to stop you."

"You wanted me to want you to stop me."

"No, I wanted to do a lot of inappropriate things to you on the—"

Oh, hell no. She did not need those images in her head. "So have you been to Hawaii before this?"

"No," he grinned, amused by her sudden subject change. "It's my first time. How about you?"

"Same."

On the quiet, dark beach, moonlight and an occasional tiki flame guiding their steps, a comfortable silence settled between them, with the waves breaking against the sand the only sound.

"Can I walk you to your room?"

She led the way in response.

"What are your plans for tomorrow?"

"Hoping to make it to the gym before breakfast tomorrow. Gianna and I are taking a helicopter tour, and will probably go shopping after that. What about you?"

"I'm thinking about signing up for surfing or snorkeling lessons. I want to spend as much time as possible in the water so I haven't really looked into anything else."

London pictured him shirtless, wet shorts clinging to his legs, his chest and abs glistening with water as he walked toward her. The fire spread and made her ache. Made her want to do something really stupid.

"Well," she stopped just a few feet from her door, just in case Gianna was waiting and watching. "I guess I'll see you around then."

"I was thinking," he said, his tone playful and friendly. "Since this is our third encounter, it kind of adds up to a first date."

"Yeah, right," she said, rolling her eyes.

"And since I'm going all in…" He trailed off,

stepping toward her with a predatory look in his eyes.

She stepped back and right into the wall. "If you—
"

"Kiss you? Oh, I'd love to."

He pulled her into his arm and waited, his lips hovering over hers, his eyes meeting hers. Hers lit up with fire, and seeing it, he wanted to stake his claim even more.

What would she do? How would she respond? Whatever the outcome, he hoped this hurt and hurt good.

He brushed his lips lightly across her right cheek, and then her left, his grip tightening when her breath caught in response. Then he gentled his hold on her and took a step back while he was still in control.

"Damn you," she said, her voice strained.

With the fire in her panties reaching wildfire status, London grabbed a fistful of his shirt and yanked him close. She pressed her mouth to his, pleased when he kissed her greedily in return.

Too caught up to be gentle, to be cautious, she nipped and tugged at his lips, swallowing every little groan and offering him one in return. She held onto his shirt like a lifeline while his hands cruised down her sides to dig into her hips.

It hurt, and it was the best pain he had ever experienced in his entire life. She was all claws and teeth, and every scratch and nip weakened the chains of reason until the wild beast he knew lurked in his soul reared its ugly head.

Mad with desire, he lifted her up, pulled her legs around his waist, and pressed into her. He knew he hit the right spot when she moaned.

"Shit. Okay. Okay. I have an idea."

He pressed kisses against her neck. "I'm mostly listening."

"We have sex, get this out of our system, and then go back to our lives once we're home."

Tony stopped. "That sounds like a trap, not an idea."

"How so?"

He released her legs so she could stand and stepped back enough to create a little space between them. He obviously would need to think through the lust-crazed fog clouding his brain.

"If I agree to that, you'll think I'm just looking for sex, then get mad as a result, and not sleep with me as punishment. If I don't agree to it, you won't sleep with me. Either way, I'm stuck with the worst case of blue balls known to man. It's a trap. A blue balls trap."

London rested her head against the wall, laughing lightly. She took a breath before she looked at him.

"It's not. I swear. Just a week of no strings attached sex."

Tony looked at her, knowing a week was not enough. "How about sex, this week and next, just to be absolutely sure we've gotten each other out of our systems, and then, at the end of the two weeks, we reevaluate, and go from there."

London bit her lip and got distracted from her thoughts when his eyes tracked the movement and seemed to darken in anticipation.

She still didn't trust him, not enough to date him, and she didn't think she would change her mind in two weeks. But if they both agreed up front that this was just sex? Well, she could do that, especially if they were on the same page about it.

"Sex only. No dates. You're obviously terrible at the

second, and seem like you'll be good at the first."

He would like to prove her wrong about the second, but knew he needed more time to do so. "You agree to revisit this conversation after two weeks and we got a deal."

"Deal."

"Fine. Your room or mine?"

"Wait, I didn't say tonight."

"I have one, maybe two condoms in my wallet. It's been…a small amount of time since my last…Anyway. We need to know if you can handle all of this before I go out and buy more tomorrow."

She choked out a laugh. "If I can handle it?"

"Exactly," he said with a cocky smile. "Which room?"

"Your room," she said, eager to wipe that smirk off his face. "I'm sharing mine with Gianna."

He took her hand and led her to the elevator. She watched him press the call button, and thought about being alone with him in that little space.

"Take the stairs."

He looked over at her, felt all logical thought leave his head when he saw her heated expression.

"Shit. Shit, shit, shit. You just ruined my entire plan."

"What plan?" She asked, following him up the stairs.

Tony took out his wallet, inspected it's contents. "I've got two condoms, thank god. First is definitely going to be hard, and fast, and rough, thanks to your dirty little mind. Elevator sex. You surprise me."

"Then you probably won't be able to handle all of this," she said calmly, even as her heart raced in anticipation.

He pulled out his key and unlocked the door. "Guess we're going to find out."

CHAPTER 6

London reached for him the moment she crossed the threshold, but he was faster, and the sudden movement sent her heart racing. His hands gripped her hips and the hard, hot length of his body pressed her against the wall just inside the entryway before the door even closed.

The light came on, triggered by the press of her body against it, and poured light over them like some erotic spotlight while the rest of the room stayed dark. They were both breathing heavy as they stared at each other.

"Hold this," he commanded, passing her the condom.

Then their lips met in a battle for dominance, nipping and biting, their tongues raging war. Gasps and moans flew like bullets while their hands tore at each other like blades.

He slid both his hands up her arms to push the thin straps over her shoulders. In the recesses of his mind, he gave thanks to whatever fashion god had created the black spaghetti strapped romper. When she pulled her arms free and the fabric hung at her waist, he yanked down her bra and greedily palmed her breasts.

London moaned against his mouth, gasped when he

bit her lower lip in response. She dove her hands under his shirt, dragging her nails across his chest as she lifted it. When he pulled away enough to tug the shirt over his head, she took stock of his flat stomach as she tugged at the button on his cotton shorts.

She wanted to touch and taste, but needed him inside her more than she wanted to breathe.

"Hurry," she panted, helping him push the shorts and boxers over his hips, and whimpered when he sprang free.

He took the condom, ripped the package open. "You're a little overdressed to be rushing me."

She solved the issue by wiggling her hips, a motion that made him fumble a bit as he slipped the condom on. He was too blind with lust to fully appreciate her naked beauty, and so he grabbed her, hoisted her up. She didn't hesitate, but wrapped her arms and legs around him for balance.

Tony moved his hands, got a good grip on her legs, and filled her to the hilt.

Their breath mingled together in a collective sigh of pleasure.

He wanted to go slow, wanted to savor this moment, one that he had dreamed of probably since he first discovered the beauty that was the female body. But the beast was free, and it had control of him, eager and anxious to claim the prize he had always denied himself before it was snatched away yet again.

Hardly believing that he was getting what he wanted, his mind absorbed and cataloged her every moan, every tremble, every little scratch she left on his back. He saw the way she bit her lips when he transitioned from hard, slow thrust to quick, shallow bursts.

He wondered which she liked best. Hoped it was slow and hard because he switched back, willing his body to drag out this pleasure as long as he could, even as he felt his orgasm drawing nearer.

Knowing she had lost the battle for dominance, London could do little more than hold on as he claimed his willing prize. How could she have known that he had this beast chained inside him? Is this why he had held back?

Mad with the pleasure he gave her, she thought she could understand why. The hands that dug into her hips felt more like hooks that she would never be free of.

And in the moment her orgasm ripped through her, she wasn't sure she wanted to be.

Watching her fall apart in his arms, he let go and joined her over the edge.

Tony held her there a moment, legs and arms trembling, heart pounding wildly in his chest as he worked to slow his breathing.

Worried that he might drop her, he summoned his remaining strength and repositioned his hands before slowly stumbling over to the bed. He sat, and then lay back on the bed, lightly stroking her back.

London curled into his side. "Down for the count. Guess I was too much for you after all."

He chuckled. "Not even close. I'm giving you a break."

"Uh huh, sure. It's okay to show a little weakness now and again."

He rolled over on top of her. "Fine. I'm going to order some food because I'm man enough to admit that I need a little fuel after that. I'm hoping you'll just stay naked in bed, but I can get you a shirt if you're feeling modest."

"I could also just put my clothes back on," she said dryly.

"Yeah, but it's much easier for me to get to you if you're only wearing my shirt. Better yet, if you're naked. I'm hoping you'll stay naked."

London rolled her eyes at the innocent smile she could just make out in the dim light. "Fine. I'll take the shirt."

"Killjoy." He looked at the clock. "Oh, but first food. Room service ends in ten minutes. What do you want?"

"Nothing. Should I remind you that this isn't a date?"

"I know." Tony picked up the phone and held it between his ear and his shoulder. "It's not date food. It's fuel for round two food."

"Fine."

Knowing Gianna would be wondering where she was, she rose from the bed to get their discarded items while he ordered. After turning on the light next to the bed, she crossed the room and gathered up everything in her arms and came back to the bed.

Tony was watching her, his eyes full of the promise of what was to come. She wondered if he really needed the food he was ordering to replenish his energy or if he was just trying to get her to stay.

Food meant waiting. Waiting meant space for conversation. Conversation meant getting to know each other. These were all of the things that she was desperate to avoid.

After he hung up, he rose from the bed and tossed open the suitcase that sat on the luggage rack. He grabbed a pair of boxers, and tossed a shirt to her with a wink and disappeared in the bathroom, leaving her alone.

She quickly slipped on his shirt before pulling her phone out. There was, of course, a string of separate text messages from Gianna, and, unfortunately, a few from Valerie through the group text.

Cringing, and not quite ready to deal with the colossal fallout of what she had just done, and what she had agreed to for the next two weeks, she sent a quick text, letting them know where she was, and promising to give all the details tomorrow. Then she put her phone on airplane mode to avoid the deluge of messages that was sure to come.

Tony stepped from the bathroom, shirtless and wearing boxers. "Can I see something?"

"Hmm?"

She started to turn to him, but he placed his hands on her shoulders to stop her. Unable to help himself, he rubbed his nose against her neck as he dropped his right hand to her hip to lift his shirt.

His, he thought, his heart pounding painfully against his chest. Distracted by the thought of claiming her, he brushed his lips against her neck and cupped her breast. She leaned back against him, a knowing smile on her lips.

"You did that on purpose," he accused.

"What are you talking about?" She asked, baffled, and completely turned on.

"Distracted me," he explained, and leaned over to search for the tattoo he thought he had seen riding on her hip. "Aha!" He read the Chinese characters, spoke in Mandarin. "London. The first character means kinship, the second, kind hearted. Do I have your kind heart to thank for tonight? You have no idea what you've given me."

She chuckled, automatically answered in Mandarin. "I don't think my heart had anything to do with this. And it feels like I've given you another boner."

When his hands tightened on her, she thought, *oh, shit.*

"You speak Mandarin?" He asked, still speaking in his home language.

Fuck. She hadn't planned on letting him know. The less they knew about each other, the easier it would be to walk away at the end of these two weeks.

She could have easily played ignorant, but hadn't considered that he spoke the language, or that she couldn't actually turn off years of study and practical use and not respond in kind. But now that he knew, the questions would follow.

"Yes, obviously," she said playfully, turning to wrap her arms around him. She slid her hands into the waistband of his boxers and nibbled on his chin. "If that was all you wanted to see, I have to say, I'm kind of disappointed."

He struggled to think past how it felt to have her hands and mouth on him. "Uh, why didn't you say anything?"

Now she flicked her tongue over his pecs. "Do you normally announce to people that you speak Mandarin?"

"No, but—"

"And why would I assume that you speak Mandarin? What if you were Japanese, like Jun? Or Vietnamese. What if you didn't even speak another language?"

London slid her hands up his back and gripped his shoulders, pulling him down so she could kiss him. He responded by pulling her against him. Wanting to further distract him, she gave him a small moan.

"Time for round two?"

Tony glanced at the clock. He had maybe fifteen to twenty minutes before the food arrived. He didn't know her body yet. Didn't know how and where she liked to be touched.

But he was most certainly going to try to get another orgasm out of her before room service knocked on the door.

Looked like the theme for tonight was hard and fast instead of the slow and easy he had hoped for.

"On your back," he demanded, his voice rough as he released her.

She lifted her eyebrows, but let him go to sit on the bed, scooting backward until she had enough space to lie down. Then her eyes widened when he knelt over her, pushing her knees out so that she was open for him.

She squeezed them shut on a surprised gasp when he tasted her with fast flicks of his tongue. Still sensitive from before, she bucked against him, pressing her hand to his head in defense against the overwhelming pleasure.

But he didn't ease up, and, adding his fingers, drove her quickly and ruthlessly to the peak until she came crashing down.

Tony looked around for his wallet, saw that she had pushed it and his pile of clothes to the side so she could lie down. Why had he thought that would be enough?

Now he had a true taste of her. It would never be enough. He would never get enough of her. Shaking with the need to be inside her, he grabbed his wallet, and then let out a stream of curses when he heard the sharp knock at the door.

He scowled down at London as she laughed. "This isn't funny."

"Oh, but it is," she said, sitting up and holding her hand out for his wallet. "I wouldn't answer the door like that. They don't need that kind of tip."

"You're going to pay for this," he warned, handing her cash for the tip.

London grinned. "I can't wait."

The scent of the food hit her stomach, made her salivate. So maybe she was hungry. They had just burned several thousand calories after all.

She exchanged the cash for the tray and after kicking the door closed, carried it to him. He took the tray and nodded to the table.

"Join me. I got a burger and fries to split. And a Dr. Pepper for you."

Surprised, she joined him at the table. "How did you know I liked Dr. Pepper?"

"You threw it in my face, remember?"

She laughed. "Oh, yeah."

"I deserved it," he said, cutting the burger in half. "You really know how to put a man in his place."

"You're welcome."

He grinned, stuffing fries in his mouth as he did. "Thank you. I don't mind. Makes it that much more rewarding when I take the reins in bed."

"What does that mean?" She picked up her drink to take a sip.

"I can't say, not yet. It's too early for that kind of thing. We'll talk more about it next week, after you've gotten used to me."

She scrunched up her nose. "If you're talking ass play, you can call this thing done."

"No, I'm not. But now that you mention it…" He looked down at her butt.

She kicked him. "No."

"Where are you shopping tomorrow?" He asked, wanting to change the subject. "Maybe I can bum a ride so I can make a trip to Costco."

"What do you need at Costco?"

"Condoms."

She paused with the burger halfway to her mouth. "Costco does not sell condoms."

"Yeah they do."

"No way."

"Why wouldn't they?"

"Because no one person needs that many condoms."

"Agree to disagree. I'll show you my receipt tomorrow. Can I get a ride or not?"

She scowled at him. "Maybe."

"I think I can turn that maybe into yes."

He stood and grabbed a fistful of his shirt she wore, then yanked her up to him.

"Time for round two."

∞∞∞∞∞∞∞∞∞

"Wakey, wakey! It's time to give us all the deets, my naughty little friend!"

London groaned, wishing she could ignore Gianna's incessant prodding. The more alert she became, the more aware she was of every little sore muscle in her body. She hadn't had sex in eight months, and couldn't remember a time when she had felt as used as she did now after breaking a dry spell. All she wanted to do was sleep and recover.

But Gianna had not so quietly woken up, moving around the room noisily until she had gotten in the shower long enough for London to doze off again. Then she was calling room service, and the silence that followed that call lasted all of fifteen minutes before Valerie arrived.

Why had she promised to tell them anything? Why was she even friends with them? And why had she promised to see Tony again? He had clearly broken her if she was questioning her friendships and her life choices.

"Alright! I'm up," she insisted after Gianna shoved her harder. She sat up, prepared to scowl, when Valerie handed her a cup of coffee. "Oh, thank god."

Valerie grinned. "I'm starving, so I'd like to move this along. You're not the only one who had a night of sex."

"Brag, brag, brag. You're lucky I love you two. Now let's go."

"Can I at least go to the bathroom first?"

Gianna scowled. "Ugh, fine."

They had room service set up breakfast on the patio, and they had even brought a folding chair so that there was enough seating for the three of them. Since the bride and groom had requested an ocean view room, and that their guests be near their suite, they were able to enjoy the sight and sounds of the water.

Seeing it, and after taking another sip of her coffee, she felt refreshed. The cobwebs cleared from her mind, she prepared herself to be grilled.

"I already told Valerie about all the stuff that has happened between you two. You know, the stuff you refused to tell us about, so she's all caught up. How the hell did you go from reluctantly talking to him to banging him?"

London talked around a piece of bacon as she began to fill them in. By the time she was done, they had devoured a mountain of pancakes and had drunk entirely too many mimosas.

"I'm so sore, but dear god I can't wait to go back. It's been so long since I've had sex this good."

"Seriously, how have I not had sex with an Asian guy yet?"

Valerie laughed. "I'll ask Jun if he has any single friends."

"I tried to get you to talk to him that night."

Gianna snorted. "Please. I saw the way you two were looking at each other when I walked in. I didn't stand a chance."

"What do you think will happen at the end of these two weeks? Sounds like he might want something more from you."

London sighed, and a little light headed from the champagne, answered honestly. "I'm terrified I might want more too."

"Why is that such a bad thing? I haven't seen the way you guys interact, but from what Gianna says, it sounds like there might be some real chemistry between you two."

"I just don't want to make the same mistakes, you know?"

Valerie nodded. "Preaching to the choir. That's how I was with Jun, so I know it's not an easy thing to do, but I have to say it. Don't worry about it."

"I don't want to get hurt again."

"If he hurts you, I'll hurt him. Literally. You won't be able to stop me this time," Gianna promised. "Brovaries before ovaries."

London laughed. "I think you meant ovaries before brovaries."

"Obviously I need more champagne. I can't think straight."

Valerie grinned as she filled their glasses, and then raised hers. "Ovaries before brovaries!"

With a clink of their glasses, they toasted in solidarity.

∞∞∞∞∞∞

Valerie and Jun's wedding invitations had also included a list of optional excursions for guests to attend along with the bride and groom.

After years and years of listening to Jun rave about the beautiful beaches he had visited throughout the world, Tony intended to spend as much of his first trip to Hawaii figuring out what it was that drove his friend to travel to beach cities. As a result, he had only agreed to join them on excursions that included the beach or going out to sea.

But now that he had met, and wanted to continue enjoying, London, he wanted to spend as much time as possible with her.

When London had mentioned in passing that she and Gianna were joining Valerie and Jun on the long and well-famed trip to Hana, he snuck into the bathroom to text Jun about joining the trip if there was still space for him.

Jun had been more than a little grateful that he had decided to attend since he was going to be the only male on the trip. He felt only a little bit guilty that he wasn't even remotely interested in spending time with his friend.

So, after rushing out to the nearest store for some hiking sandals, Tony sat in the front seat of the van while Jun drove and the women chatted in the back.

He enjoyed hearing her voice, the soft rise and fall of it whenever she spoke. He noticed that she mostly kept to herself, chiming in on Gianna and Valerie's conversation when it seemed to suit her mood as they cruised along the windy roads.

When they got out to explore, she often trailed behind, phone in hand, quietly drinking in the view.

At first he thought that maybe it was because of him, but as he watched her and her interactions with her friends, he realized that this was also who she was. Even after two nights of uninhibited sex, it intrigued him that he still had so much more to learn about her.

She didn't exactly embrace his presence with open arms, but she didn't outright ignore him like she had before their arrangement. She was friendly and didn't seem to mind if he commented on something her friends said. And the heated looks she sent him when she caught him watching her let him know that he wasn't the only one looking forward to tonight.

Jun bumped into him, jarring his attention away from London. "Can you give me a hand with the bags? The ladies are ready to eat."

"Yeah, sure." Tony followed Jun up the stairs that led to the picnic area of Wai'anapanapa State Park. "So where would this rank on your list of favorite beaches?"

Jun jiggled his keys in his pocket as he thought. "Man, that's a tough one. The black sand is so unique, I might have to put it high on the list."

"Number one for me for sure. This beach makes the trip worth it."

"Just the beach, huh?" Jun asked, slanting him a look with a sly grin on his face. "London didn't have anything to do with it? I swear every time I turn around I see you staring at her."

Tony chuckled nervously. "That obvious, huh?"

"I didn't know you were interested in black women," he shared. "When did this start?"

"Probably middle school," he confessed.

"No shit? All the times we've gone out together, I never saw you look or talk to any woman who wasn't Asian."

He had good reasons for that, he thought, as Jun stopped in front of the van. But he wasn't quite ready to share them.

"Because I never did. Never thought I had a chance, so I didn't even try."

"But you're going to try with London. What changed?"

"Even as diverse as Sacramento is, you and I both know that it's usually Asian and white women who are interested in us. When you and Valerie started dating, I thought, damn, that lucky son of a bitch caught a unicorn. I'm not going to lie, it took me a while to move past the jealousy."

"Shit, Tony. Is that the real reason you haven't been around?"

He leaned back against the car. "I'm embarrassed to say it, but yeah."

"Well, fuck." Jun mirrored him. "I don't know what to say."

"There's nothing to say. That's my hang up, not yours. Anyway, I got over it. Then I met London. It was the first time I've ever looked at a black woman and saw her looking back at me. We both got there early, so I didn't know that she was Valerie's friend and I…"

Tony shook his head. "I fucked up, basically. Now I have a chance to fix it. I think."

"Gotta take that first step then, man." Jun pushed off the car and moved to the back. "Gotta make something happen."

"Something already happened, though it's more her idea than mine."

Jun reached in the van, then pulled back as he thought about what Tony said.

"Valerie was furiously texting the night we got here, and then the next morning, she ditched me to go have breakfast with London and Gianna." He gasped. "Holy shit! You're sleeping with London? How long has this been going on?"

Tony looked around, making sure the girls hadn't come looking for them since they were taking so long.

"It just happened. I was trying to explain why I fucked up at Ella's, and…things just kind of exploded between us. But she wants to keep it strictly as sex only for the next week and a half. I'm hoping I can convince her not to drop me when we get to the end of it."

"Oh, man, I did not see that coming. If Gianna had put those kinds of stipulations on something like this, I wouldn't have blinked. But London? That surprises me. Of the three of them, she's definitely the quiet one, and seems the most level headed."

"I'm starting to see the quiet, and even the way she laid out this whole thing, it's pretty level headed, even if it might work out to my disadvantage. Maybe you can try to casually get some info about her out of Valerie that I can use to my advantage?"

Jun snorted. "Yeah, I'll get back to you in like a

week. You're not the only one getting laid this week."

"Anything you can get, man. I'd appreciate it."

"Yeah, yeah, yeah. I get it. She's your unicorn."

CHAPTER 7

On a cloudless, sunny day, Tony watched his childhood friend marry the love of his life.

They stood at the altar holding hands, beaming at each other as the ocean lapped quietly at the shore behind them. Valerie's dress was all beautiful and elegant lace up top while the bottom was a solid, simple fabric that flowed around her ankles.

He knew next to nothing about bridal fashion, but thought the look suited her perfectly. And Jun, in his crisp light gray suit, complimented her perfectly.

After the ceremony, he hung in the background with the rest of the wedding party since the groomsmen and bridesmaids had already taken their respective group photos.

He watched while the bride and groom took pictures with their family members. He envied Jun more than a little when his mother, small tears in her eyes, embraced Valerie, and his father gave Jun a congratulatory handshake.

If only his parents could be that accepting. Knowing it was a stretch, knowing what he was risking in pursuing London, his head began to fill with doubt, chasing away the joy he felt for his friend. Then he heard London chatting away with Gianna and the guilt made him feel sick to his stomach.

Needing to get away for a moment, he tried his best to fix his face and turned to the group.

"Hey, I'm going to get a drink. Can I get you ladies anything?"

London looked over at him, wondering why he didn't look directly at them. "I'm okay. Thanks though."

"Same," Gianna said, and watched him walk away. "Is he okay? He looked like he was going to hurl."

"He did look off."

"Go find out," she said, giving London a light shove in his direction.

"Pass. I'm sure he'll work it out."

"Fine. Then tell me about the taller, muscular, younger, and much hotter version of Ruben over there. Those biceps look like weapons," she said, checking him out and quite enjoying what she was seeing. "He seems so familiar. I'm sure we've met him before but I can't remember when."

"That's Hunter. Val's cousin. Your math tutor for six months your sophomore year in high school."

Gianna's mouth dropped open. "That shy towering twig turned into that?"

London chuckled. "Interested?"

"Surprised," she admitted, still watching him.

London wiggled her eyebrows at her. "And interested."

Grinning, she snagged Gianna's arm and, ignoring her friend's protests, dragged her across the beach to where Hunter stood.

Dressed in a thin, white cotton dress shirt and black tie, Hunter looked slightly uncomfortable. London suspected, judging from his muscular build, that he spent more time in the gym than in places that required such formal attire.

"Hey, Hunter," she called.

He turned to them and his back went ramrod straight when they stopped in front of him. His brown eyes passed briefly over Gianna before meeting London's.

"Hey, London. Good to see you again."

"Same. You remember, Gianna, right?"

"From high school, right? Didn't realize you three were still a thing."

Gianna sent him a flirtatious smile. "Some things never change, ya know? What have you been up to since then?"

He shrugged. "This and that."

Gianna's eyebrows flew up. "So mysterious. I see that hasn't changed much either."

"Guess not," he said, looking over at the bride and groom as they posed with his aunt and uncle.

"So," she drawled. "Do you live in Sac? Or here and there?"

Hunter glanced over at her briefly. "Here and there."

"So. Amazing."

London grinned. "I thought Valerie said you weren't coming."

"The job I was on wrapped up early, so I made it. Got in last night."

"What a nice surprise," Gianna said, smiling up at him. "So we'll see you at the reception then?"

"Yep."

Gianna pursed her lips. "I'm going to get a drink after all. Want anything, London?"

"No, I'm good," she said, grinning in amusement.

"How about you, Hunter? Want anything?"

"No."

Gianna shrugged before walking away. Hunter slid his hands into his pockets.

"How are your parents?"

"They're good. Looking forward to retirement."

"Good for them, even if that means more work for you." She bumped him with her shoulder. "You still don't like her, huh?"

"Who? Gianna? I don't even know her."

"You guys rode the bus together for nearly two years, and she always talked to you. You tutored her, which ended up being a really big deal for her, by the way."

He titled his head toward her. "Okay."

"And yet, you hated her in high school."

"In high school. When I was a child," he said, shifting his weight. "I'm long past anything I felt for anyone in high school, hate or otherwise."

One of the wedding coordinators informed the group that they could move into the dining room so they turned and walked back toward the resort.

London bit her lip to hide her grin. "Didn't seem like it to me. You were awfully short with her."

"Like I said, I don't even know her. Why don't you tell me about that guy who is drooling all over you?"

"I don't because I'm talking about you and Gianna."

Hunter shook his head. "Nothing to talk about."

"Alright," she said, holding her hands up in defeat. "But I'm warning you. You keep that wall up, she's going to wonder why, and she'll keep at you until she knocks it down to get the answer."

"Gianna couldn't care less about me," he said flatly.

"And the feeling is mutual. I'm going to sit with the Halls. See you around."

Unconvinced, she stared after him as he walked inside the small dining room. There were four tables elegantly dressed in mint and white tablecloths. Instead of flowers for centerpieces, a single lit candle with a variety of shells around its base stood in the middle of the table.

Since there were only about twenty people who had attended the wedding, London knew she would end up sitting with Tony.

She glanced around the room and, sure enough, Tony was seated at a table and talking to Gianna. She assumed the empty chair between them was for her. With a resigned sigh, she joined them.

Feeling more like himself, Tony draped his arm over the back of London's chair. Needing the connection, and the reassurance that what they had was real, if only temporary, he brushed his fingers over the back of her neck. She slanted him a look, but thankfully didn't try to stop him.

He wanted to get her alone. Not just for the sex, though the way that mint colored dress clung to her every curve made it difficult to think of little else.

He wanted an opportunity to get to know her, and for her to know him. They had more time together on that first night than they had during the ones that followed.

There really hadn't been any time for just the two of them during the day, which ultimately was exactly what she wanted. And so she came to his room late at night and was gone before sunrise, giving him no opportunity to get to learn anything about her.

When he agreed to no strings attached sex, he

figured they would have some time to talk. But they seemed to always manage to fill the down time between sex with some hot and heavy petting that eventually led right back to sex. She must really think he had a one-track mind.

It didn't help that she still didn't trust him. He understood and respected her caution given how poorly he handled things with her initially.

Her lack of trust was his own damn fault, and he had no right complaining about the consequences. He knew that earning it back would take time, but he was worried that he didn't have enough of it before she walked away from him.

He wasn't getting anywhere feeling sorry for himself. He had to use the time that he had to make some progress. Thanks to Jun and Valerie's nuptials, they had spent a lot of time together today.

He had walked with her down the aisle on the beach, posed with her for photos, and now she was letting him touch her while they watched the newlyweds have their first dance. He needed to strengthen their connection, and now was probably better than later.

"Is it weird to see your childhood friend getting married like it is for me?" He whispered in her ear, his hand pressing her just a little bit closer to him.

"Hadn't thought of it, but I guess it is," London answered, smiling at the couple.

"Jun was such a little shit in first grade. I can't believe how much he's grown up."

She slanted him a look. "And I suppose you were an angel."

He rubbed his nose against hers. "I'm only a demon in bed. The rest of the time, I'm the perfect angel."

She rolled her eyes and sat up just a little to create the space he only just closed. "Oh, boy."

Tony grinned. "Ask Jun. I was the perfect kid back then. We had this friend, Brian, and Jun and I were super protective of him. He had cystic fibrosis, and some of the kids could be little shits to him, so I kind of took on the role of gentle, guardian angel. But Jun? Demon avenger. If anyone so much as gave Brian a dirty look, Jun was all over them. I think he just liked the excuse of picking fights."

"Jun doesn't seem like he has a mean bone in his body."

"Only certain things bring it out, and defending Brian was one of them. When my family moved to Sacramento, Jun took his duties even more seriously since he was riding solo. I guess that's when he started to grow up a little."

Interested in his story, she divided her attention between him and her plate after it was served. "Do you guys still keep in touch with Brian?"

"He passed away, unfortunately. Some stupid shit that could have been avoided had he gotten the right care. But he's why Jun and I reconnected. Jun's parents, who were friends with Brian's, let my parents know about Brian, so I was able to make it to the funeral. Jun and I reconnected there and made a pact in Brian's memory to donate regularly to Disability Rights California in hopes that it helps someone get what they need and deserve."

"I'm sorry for your loss," she said, placing her hand gently on his leg. "I think Brian would appreciate what you're doing for people with disabilities."

He shrugged it off, but enjoyed the warmth of her touch. "Its just money. People like you, you're doing the real work."

"Yes, but you also use your position to make positive change. Frank made a pretty substantial donation because you pointed him in our direction."

"Pft. He was trying to buy his way into your bed. I don't think he gives two shits about people with disabilities."

London shook her head. "That may be true, but the end result is the same. This was the third year that someone paid for us to go to the Kings game. It doesn't always mean a donation to the agency as well, but it definitely means a lot to some of my coworkers to know that someone values their work enough to treat them to a game. It revitalizes them, and makes them fight harder. You made that happen, so what you do is just as important as what I do."

He wrinkled his nose, not really buying it. "I've been with the Kings…wow, it'll be six years in a few months. Damn. Promoted to Marketing Manager two years ago. How long have you been with DRC? Why didn't I see you last year?"

"Only two years, but I volunteered there when I was getting my masters at Sac State, which is why they hired me. I don't think they offered me a ticket last year since I was still new."

"You're a Sac State alum too? When were you there?"

"Aren't there a lot of Sac State alums in Sacramento?" She asked with a little laugh. "I was there five years ago."

"I got my MBA six years ago, so I just missed you. What did you study?"

Her eyes swung briefly toward Gianna before she answered. "Teaching English to speakers of other languages."

There were so many more questions that he wanted to ask. So many more things he wanted to know. But this was the most she had shared with him, and he could see that she was ready to shut him down.

Biting back the frustration, and refusing to acknowledge the hurt, he slid to the edge of his chair.

"That's pretty cool. Do me a favor? Make sure they leave me a piece of cake?"

London nodded in response, then sighed in relief when he left the table.

"And I thought I was the drama queen."

London looked over at Gianna. "What?"

"You're sighing like he asked you your deepest, darkest secrets," she accused, her tone conveying her disappointment. "The guy just wants to get to know you."

"Eavesdropping much?"

Gianna sent her a dirty look. "There are what, twenty people here? I heard you whether or not I wanted to. Can you be less of a dick?"

London leaned closer to her and whispered. "Can you lower your voice?"

"Why are you treating him like that?"

"Because this isn't a date!" She lowered her voice again. "We don't need to do the 'get to know you' crap."

"You'd share what you studied in college with a perfect stranger without a second thought. Dating or not, it wouldn't kill you to treat the guy you're screwing better than you would a stranger."

"I'm not…that's not…damn it," London said with a frown, facing the truth.

"Yeah, you marinate on that." Gianna sat back, then

beamed over at Tony when he returned. "Are you sailing with us tomorrow, Tony?"

He sat and picked up his fork. "Oh, yeah. Been looking forward to it since Jun suggested it. You guys ever been sailing before? Holy shit, this cake is delicious."

London picked up her own fork, realizing that she had been so caught up in her conversation with Gianna that she hadn't noticed that the wait staff had delivered the cake.

"I've been sailing in Italy, but I think this will be a first for London and Val."

"Ugh. I hope I don't get seasick," London groaned.

The lights dimmed suddenly and strobe lights kicked on just as happy music began playing. Jun and Valerie took to the small dance floor again, inviting others to join them, as they ramped up the celebration.

Gianna tugged London with her, leaving Tony alone at the table. He watched, grinning, as their bodies swayed and moved to the music.

She was relaxed now. Carefree. Smiling and laughing as though that was what she always did. He liked seeing this side of her, and hoped one day she might be that way with him.

Then Gianna marched determinedly toward him and yanked him up to pull him onto the dance floor.

"Going to the ladies room. Keep my gal company, will you?"

Tony grinned. "With pleasure."

Grinning, Gianna strode off the dance floor and out the dining room. Stepping off to the side, she stuck her head back in to look inside just as Hunter was coming out.

Her face struck the pure, solid muscle of his chest

as they collided. She wasn't sure if she was dizzy from the impact or from the tantalizing hit of his cologne that was now likely embedded in her nostrils.

He gripped her arm roughly as he stumbled for balance, and she nearly toppled onto him again as a result. She brought her hand up to his chest to right herself, felt the steel of his body and the hammering of his heart.

"Christ. Watch where you're going," he demanded, his tone conveying his annoyance, and released her arm as if she had burned him.

"Um, my ears must be ringing from being struck by solid rock," she said, rubbing them for effect. "It sounds like you're blaming me for you nearly knocking me over."

"It's not my fault that you're not paying attention to where you're going."

Gianna blinked at him. "Pretty sure in situations like this, no one is at fault, but people usually check on each other to make sure everyone is okay instead of berating them."

"You're fine, obviously," he said, shoving his hands in his pockets.

"And you're the perfect gentleman," she said dryly.

"Look, I know you're used to guys falling all over themselves to talk to you—"

"Let me stop you right there," she insisted, her voice going ripe with anger. "Because if you finish that statement, if you blame your callousness toward my well being on my looks, I will, without any hesitation, make you regret it."

Hunter felt something like shame burn in his belly. "That's not what I was trying to say."

"How smart of you," she said hotly. "Now if you'll

excuse me, I need to see about this bruise that's probably forming on my face. Since you slammed in to me."

When she turned and walked away, his guilt carried him after her.

"You're not really hurt. Are you?"

"Your chest is as hard as I imagine your head is, so I think it's worth investigating."

"Shit. Wait. Let me see."

He grabbed her arm again, all but yanked her around to face him. As she checked the urge to go for a standing arm lock in self-defense, she wondered if he understood the concept of gentle. When his other hand took hold of her chin, she was convinced that he didn't.

"You know, manhandling me will only make it worse," she said, trying to pull away.

"Hold still," he demanded, turning her face so he could see. "A little red, but I doubt you'll bruise."

Their eyes met, and seconds became minutes as warmth from where he held her chin traveled through her body until it burst from the tips of her fingers and toes. There was a very distinct and strange shift in the air, and her heart rate sped up in response.

His eyes flicked down to her lips, then snapped back up just as quickly. Before she could decipher what was happening to her, to them, his eyes frosted over. They turned hard and angry. He dropped his hand and took a huge step back.

"You're—you'll be okay."

"Yeah…thanks, doctor."

Gianna turned and walked to the bathroom. Inside, she stuck her hands in cold water to try to shock her system into restarting and stared at her reflection. She was a little wide-eyed and her cheeks were slightly pink.

Seeing as that had been the most bizarre interaction that she had ever had with another human being before, she thought she could have looked worse for the wear.

There was something up with Hunter Hall, and the reckless part of her wanted to find out what that was.

Since she was feeling a little off balance by the whole thing, she decided that drinking until she forgot was a much safer course of action.

∞∞∞∞∞∞∞

It was two in the morning when London and Gianna finally made their way back to their room. Not late by most party girl standards, but they were quickly approaching twenty-four hours of being awake since their day had started at five am.

After the reception ended, Gianna had insisted on going to the bar. There had been music, and guests from other weddings, so there had been people to talk to and things to see.

While Gianna could thrive for hours off the energy she got just from being with and around people, London must have finally looked enough like the walking dead for Gianna to take pity on her.

"You know," Gianna pointed out as they rode the elevator to Tony's floor. "You're about to go have some incredible sex that will probably keep you up for hours."

London chuckled sleepily. "I'll be back down in an hour, and sleep like the dead."

"Lucky bitch," she said without malice as they stepped out of the elevator.

London stumbled after her. "You really don't need

to go with me. Go back to the room and sleep."

"Sweetie, you're drunk with exhaustion," she pointed out, wrapping an arm around London's waist as they walked.

"Ugh. It's true. Let's go back to our room. I don't want to fall asleep here."

Gianna only grinned as she knocked on Tony's door.

"You bitch," London said with a scowl. "You did this on purpose."

Still grinning, Gianna walked away as soon as she heard the door handle turn.

Though his eyes were slightly red from the same exhaustion, Tony greeted her with a smile and pulled her inside.

"You want to rest for a bit?" He asked, pressing kisses to her neck.

"Yes. No," she said, her brain fuzzy with sleep. "A soda. With ice. That will wake me up."

He cupped her chin in one hand to get a good look at her. "You look exhausted, London. We don't have to—"

"I want to," she interrupted, her words almost like a plea. "I've wanted you to touch me all day."

He kissed her lightly on the lips, unable to resist such a confession. "Okay. I'll be right back."

Tony grabbed the ice bucket and a few dollars from his wallet. He flipped the security latch open so that he wouldn't have to bring his room key before slipping into sandals.

He really hoped she stayed awake. She wasn't the only one who was eager to be touched. Being with her was quickly becoming vital to his survival.

And maybe, just maybe, her confession meant that

he was softening her defenses.

Moving quickly down the hall, he purchased a soda from the vending machine and filled the bucket with ice. As he was making his way back down the hall, the elevator doors slid open and Gianna stepped off.

"Gianna?"

She turned to look at him and held up a bag. "I brought her clothes for tomorrow."

He blinked. "She's going to stay the whole night?"

"I guarantee you that she's already passed out, but she'll appreciate the soda in the morning."

He sighed. "Damn. Thanks though."

"One thing you should know," she said, pulling the bag back as he reached for it. "I'm currently working towards my second-degree black belt in karate and while I've made a commitment to only use my knowledge in protection and self defense, I take the protection of my friend's heart very, very seriously."

Tony could only stare as she stepped closer to him. Having only seen Gianna smile, her eyes full of mirth, the dark figure before him emanated a power that left him a little shook.

"If you hurt her, I will hurt you. Pursuing London means you agree to this arrangement. Understood?"

He gulped and nodded in response.

"Good!" She smiled brightly and handed him the bag. "Have fun!"

He blinked again, caught off guard by the sudden shifts in her mood and personality. It made her all the scarier.

Tony sighed and walked back to his room, not happy to have one more problem on his plate. But when he slipped inside and found London sleeping peacefully in his bed, everything but her melted away.

Quiet as he could, he replaced the security latch and shut the door. He placed the soda and bucket of ice on the bedside table, kicked his shoes off, and eased into bed.

She didn't wake when he pulled her into him and breathed in her soft, floral scent. At peace, he closed his eyes and gave into exhaustion.

Two hours later, Tony propped himself up on his elbow and stared down at London as she slept. Despite the fact that he was still tired, he was too turned on knowing that she was in the bed with him to actually fall into a deep sleep.

It was four in the morning now, and he couldn't wait to touch her any longer. Leaning down, he placed feather light kisses on her neck, whispered her name. She stirred, unwittingly wiggling her butt against him. He groaned, thinking he might burst if he didn't do something about the hard on he had all night.

"London, I need you to wake up now." He placed his hand on her hip to hold her in place as he rocked against her. "London. Wake up."

She grunted, stretched, and then tried to roll onto her back only to realize his chest was pressed against her back. She blinked in confusion and looked around.

"Shit. Did I fall asleep?"

"Yeah, a while ago," he told her. He flicked his tongue over the curve where her neck met her shoulder and made her squirm. "The ship is set to sail in two hours, so you've got to get up. How are you feeling?"

"I'm okay. A little thirsty. For water."

He chuckled as the hand on her hip worked to slide her bridesmaid dress up. "No hangover?"

"No, I didn't drink that much. I'm fine," she lied. She was feeling anything but fine. Her heart was racing so fast it was making her light headed. "I should get going, so I can get ready."

"Okay," he said softly, slipping his hand between her legs. "But after."

"Tony, we don't have time for this," she said on a groan when he pushed aside her panties to stroke her. Her leg lifted to give him better access. "I need to get ready."

"After," he promised, slipping a finger inside her. "God, you're so wet. I need you. I've been waiting all night."

"Then hurry," she moaned.

But he just kept stroking and playing with her, pressing kisses to her neck while she bucked against his hand. He slipped his other hand under her so he could grab and knead her breast.

She felt deliciously dirty, fully clothed in her bridesmaid dress as he pleasured her. In the recesses of her mind it alarmed her how fast he learned to exploit her body. He knew what spot on her neck made her unravel just a little bit, and that he could make her fall apart if he stroked her exactly the way he was now.

And when to pull back before she did.

While she groaned in protest, Tony rolled over on his back, snatched the condom off the side table and ripped the package open. He was rolling it on when she started to turn to lay on her back.

"Don't move," he demanded, scooting behind her. He hooked his arm behind her knee to hold up her leg and slid himself against her wet heat. "I was thinking about this all night."

Then he slipped inside her. Slow at first, letting her adjust, and taking the edge off the desperate need that had begun to well up inside of him. When he was sure he wouldn't explode, he increased his pace, driving fast and hard into her, his eyes crossing as the pleasure began to overwhelm him.

His free hand came around her again, but this time close to her neck so that he could turn her head to his to cover his mouth with hers. She moaned into his mouth and placed her hand on his arm, worried that in this wild moment he might choke her.

Something dark lit in his eyes as they met hers. His grip tightened a bit, testing her. It wasn't enough to choke her, but instead sent an unreasonable and dark thrill racing through her heart.

She realized then that she was completely at his mercy, and if she didn't get a handle on what was happening between them, she always would be.

Tony held her there, his eyes hard on hers, one arm around her neck, the other holding her leg up as he fucked her.

"Touch yourself. Make yourself come."

She whimpered, but couldn't fight the pull of the erotic moment. She was wound so tight that it took no more than a few tentative strokes of her clit before she did as he commanded.

"Ah, London," he groaned, his movements becoming more erratic as his own orgasm overtook him. "That was so fucking hot."

She moaned when he pulled out, her every nerve still on alert. "That was…"

"Too much?" He asked, tightening his grip around her neck for a brief second to indicate the choke. Then he wrapped that arm around her waist. "I should have asked….I just…"

"Completely lost your shit?"

He pressed his forehead against the back of her

neck. "Yeah. That's the thing I was planning to talk to you about next week. I should have asked before I did it."

"That doesn't sound like an apology."

Shit. He tried to force out the words, and then stopped when she laughed at him.

"You're not sorry, not even a little bit." Why did she find that hot? "I didn't realize…I've never…"

Hopeful, Tony scooted back, pulling her towards him until she lay on her back. "Did you like it?"

London bit her lip as she looked up at him. "I didn't hate it."

"There's a but in there. That's okay. We can revisit it later." He leaned down to kiss her before rolling away and off the bed. "We should get dressed."

When he held up a bag she recognized as hers, she blinked in confusion. "You brought my stuff up here?"

"Yes and no. You asked me to get you a soda and ice. On my way back, Gianna was getting off the elevator to bring me your bag."

London shook her head, but walked over to take the bag. Looking inside, she found the bathing suit and dress she had set out yesterday morning for their sailing trip today.

Since they had to get up so early, she wanted everything ready to go, knowing that she was likely to have a late night with Tony. It turned out to be an early morning with him instead.

She sighed. "I'm going to kill her."

"I'll help. I had the worst case of blue balls before I woke you up," he went into the bathroom and started the shower. "Let's hop in."

She looked at him, then the clock and back again. "We really, really don't have time for that."

Tony laughed, appreciating where her thoughts went. "And that's why the water is cold," he said, and then pulled her into the shower with him.

CHAPTER 8

He was exhausted when he finally made it home, the consequence of long days in the sun, and even longer nights of sex.

They had returned from Hawaii Friday night and he slept for nearly twelve hours before he forced himself out of bed. He was honestly dreading his next move, but it was, he knew, something that had to be done.

So he had all but begged Jun to meet him at his parent's restaurant, promising to give him all the details on how everything had unfolded between him and London. And purposefully failing to mention what else he had planned.

New Sun Restaurant was located off of Freeport in South Sacramento, and had been owned and operated by his parents since they moved from San Francisco some twenty years ago.

Mie Yu, a petite powerhouse, ran the floor with a friendly smile and a critical eye, while Huan Cheng dished up his Chinese dishes in the kitchen like a general going to war.

Tony had spent much of his childhood either serving and bussing tables, or cleaning and playing sous chef in the kitchen. But much more of his time had been playing translator.

From advertisements to permit applications, and everything in between, he had played a major role in those early days making sure the English made sense.

His parents had eventually found someone they could trust with the business and financial aspects of the restaurant, but, wanting to foster his interest in it, they ran everything through him first.

Some would say that he had a lot on his shoulders at the age of ten, but he knew it was the typical reality for American born children of immigrants.

Ultimately, it led him to Sacramento State University where he obtained his bachelors and his masters in Business Administration. After graduating, he spent the next three years building his resume at marketing companies before he landed a position with the marketing team for the NBA's Sacramento Kings. He hadn't looked back since.

But what he was about to do next was much more of a greater challenge than anything he had ever done in his life. And so with his conscience weighing heavily on him, he invited Jun and Oliver to his parent's restaurants.

Oliver was dying to know what had happened between him and London, and Jun just wanted to know what was going on.

Tony hoped that by the end of their conversation, he might be more prepared to address the problem of his parents.

Oliver leaned back in his chair, completely stuffed. "Damn, man. I mean, it's about time, but I still can't believe you finally did it."

"What? It's about time…what does that mean?" Tony asked.

Oliver sat up and looked around. Lowering his

voice, he said, "Oh you thought I didn't know that you are into black chicks?"

Tony's eyes widened. "How did you know?"

Oliver shrugged. "You get this dopey look of longing whenever you see one. Honestly, I'm surprised your parents don't know already."

"I feel like I'm missing something," Jun chimed in. "Besides learning you're into black chicks, what else am I missing?"

"Yeah," Tony began, slanting a nervous look at Jun. "I brought you here because I'm hoping you can help me with my parents. They aren't as open minded as yours are."

"Open minded about what?" Then it clicked. "Wait. Are you fucking serious?"

Tony nodded.

Baffled, Jun leaned forward. "Like how bad are we talking here? Ignore you for months 'open minded' or dead to me 'open minded'?"

"Dead to me 'open minded.' I think the only thing I heard from my dad in high school was 'Date a Chinese girl or we'll disown you'."

"Holy shit. Then why the hell did you sleep with London?"

He ran his hands over his head and face. "Because I couldn't keep walking away like she didn't affect me. Because she offered me what I've always wanted, and I was too weak to say no."

"You got it bad, man," Oliver said.

"You're screwed. How the hell am I supposed to help you?"

"We just gotta rip the bandage off, yeah?" Oliver asked, not truly believing that Tony's parents would disown him over this. "Mrs. Yu! Tony's got a girlfriend.

She's black. Is that bad?"

Tony stared at him in horror, while Jun looked on in shock. Mie approached the table, her sharp eyes focused on Tony as she moved. She came to a stop and turned to face Jun.

"How was wedding?" Her English was thick with her accent, even after all these years.

Jun swallowed audibly. "G-great."

"You have pictures?"

"Yes." When Mei held out her hand, Jun quickly retrieved his phone and pulled up some photos before handing it over.

"Hmm. She pretty." She returned his phone. "You go now."

"Uh, yep." Jun stood immediately, sending Tony a pitiful glance. "Let's go, Oliver."

"But he drove—"

"Yep. But it's time to go."

Since the weekend lunch rush was over, Mei could sit and relax, knowing her team could handle what few customers they had.

Tony felt like he was ten again. Palms sweaty and heart racing, he struggled to keep his eyes on her when he just wanted to look away.

"Is this true?" She asked in Mandarin.

"Not exactly. We…she…she is black. I like her, but we're not dating."

"Why not? Does she not like you or something?"

He blinked, not expecting that question. "She does, she just doesn't—you're not mad?"

"Disappointed," she said with a sigh, rising to stack the dishes the boys had used. "The woman I've been trying to set you up with, she's black. I really wanted you two to be together."

He gaped at her, sitting there silently until she walked away with the dishes.

"Wait. Wait. Wait. But Bà—"

She put the dishes in the bussing station. "Yes, Bà will be a problem. You let me worry about that."

"But I thought—"

"Have I ever said that I would disown you if you didn't choose a Chinese girl?" Mei came back to sit beside him. "Have you ever heard me use those words?"

Tony shook his head. "Bà always said it, but I just assumed you both felt that way."

"Do you remember that first summer you told your friends that you worked here? You were fifteen, and many of your classmates came in. Girls of all races. I noticed that you looked at them a lot differently than the Chinese girls I pushed at you. And as you got older, working here on weekends during Chinese New Year, it was the same. You never looked at the Chinese women the way you did the others.

"I come from China, where the only choice is Chinese. When I came here, I chose Chinese because that was all I knew. I didn't see that here in America there are many races, many choices. I didn't see it until I realized you did. And so I accepted that when you chose someone for yourself one day, she might not be Chinese."

She rose again, pulled a towel from her apron and began wiping the table. "Now, go on. I have much to do before dinner, and don't have time to sit around with you. Go."

Mei shooed him out the door, and hoped she lifted the weight from his shoulders.

Tony found his friends waiting on the sidewalk

when he exited the restaurant. Jun looked at him in surprise then looked dramatically down the street.

"I was expecting to see an ambulance, but you have somehow avoided physical harm." Jun noted, checking for marks. "That stunned look on your face though…what the hell happened?"

"She knew," he said, walking to the parking lot. "Not only did she know, but she's been trying to set me up with a black chick."

Oliver laughed. "Isn't that some shit?"

"Gives a whole new meaning to mother knows best!" Jun said, grinning and slapping Tony on the back. "You went from zero to two options in the span of a week. Who is this girl, and why didn't you go out with her?"

"I think it's the girl who connected them with that finance guy who helped them get a better loan and interest rate for the restaurant." Tony unlocked his Subaru and climbed inside. "I never met her. I always brush my mom off when it comes to women. I assumed she was trying to set me up with a Chinese girl like she always has."

"Big mistake. Huge," Oliver said from the backseat.

"I can't believe this whole time you've been worried about your parents for no reason."

"I still have one parent to worry about," he said as his stomach plummeted. "My dad doesn't know. My mom says he'll be a problem."

"Damn. What are you going to do?" Oliver asked. "What if things between you and London get serious?"

Tony sighed. "I'll just have to cross that bridge when I get to it."

"Or burn it," Jun said quietly.

That certainly was an option, and he was suddenly

afraid that every bridge would burn if he didn't get it right.

∞∞∞∞∞∞∞

Hours later, Tony still struggled to recover from the shock of his mother's admission. He was incredibly grateful that the conversation hadn't gone down like he had envisioned, but he was still wrapping his head around how it had.

Knowing that he had his mother's blessing at least was a great weight off his shoulders, and freed up mental space that he wanted to dedicate to making London fall in love with him.

It shocked him less to be thinking about love.

He didn't love her. But he thought he could, eventually. And since the idea didn't freak him out, he was just going to go with it. Still, the task was definitely easier said than done.

She didn't trust him, and was against dating him. And to complicate matters even more, he had absolutely no idea how to make a woman fall in love with him.

He hoped that what he had planned for tonight would be the first step in the right direction.

Tony took stock of his apartment. Mahogany cabinets lined the far wall, interrupted by stainless steel appliances. A Keurig coffee maker was the only thing that sat on white granite countertops that complimented the cabinet colors.

A bar style island with a woodblock top served as the only dining table space. He adjusted the two candles he had glowing there to make space for the platter of salami and cheese he planned to set out later.

He popped open the bottle of red wine to let it breathe and set it back down next to two wine glasses.

On the other side of the island was his living room. A fake fireplace was displayed on the large flat screen that sat above a wall mounted black television stand. It also held an assortment of lit candles.

He had pushed a rectangular shaped coffee table under the TV stand so they would have plenty of space on the blanket he laid out in front of a long gray couch.

He turned the lights down low, and thought he had all the right touches of romance. He was almost positive the set up would freak her out, but hoped he could fool her into believing he was romancing her for kinky sex and not because he was really trying to win her heart.

At the knock at the door, he drew in a deep breath before moving across the room to answer it.

She wrapped her arms around him the moment she crossed the threshold and pressed her mouth to his. When she tried to push him backward, he placed both hands on her arms to keep her there.

"Hi," he said, sliding a hand down to take hers. He used the other to shut and lock the door. "This dress gives me…ideas."

London laughed as he led her inside. The view caught her attention first. Located on the corner of 8th and J Street in downtown, the wall of windows afforded him a spectacular view of the Cesar Chavez Plaza. Though it was dark outside, the streetlights and traffic that flowed by made for an exciting light show.

Because she was so focused on the view, it took her a minute to notice the candles and dimmed lights. The wood burning fire on his television screen.

She stopped and blinked, unprepared for the

romantic atmosphere. She ordered the little flutter in her belly to go away before she looked at him.

"What the hell is all this?"

Tony slipped behind her, pressed a kiss to her neck. "Well, I was thinking, since we've only got seven more days of this."

"Six."

"Okay, six," he conceded, giving her a light nip. "Six days for me to carry out every erotic little fantasy I've had about you since we met."

London narrowed her eyes. "This feels pretty heavy on the romance and—"

"Good, good," he said, flicking his tongue over her neck the way she liked. "My plan is working."

"Look, Tony—"

"Yes, let's look." He pushed her forward until they stood in front of his window. "Just keep looking."

"What are you doing?" She asked when he pressed her into the glass and lifted up her dress. "Tony, someone might see us."

"Yes," he said, his voice low and thick as his hand dove into her panties to touch. "Well, probably not. But in my fantasy, they can see. You're going to let them watch what I do to you."

London moaned, unbelievably turned on, even as her heart raced in trepidation. "Tony…"

"Shh. I'll make it up to you with a little romance afterwards."

When he was done with her, he carried her to the couch and set her down. Heart still pounding, London leaned back, grateful for a moment alone when he left for the bathroom.

She looked around the room, terrified to stay. Terrified to leave. That he had gone through so much trouble to romance her with the candlelight and cheesy fake fire was alarming. She saw now that there were two wine glasses waiting to be filled with the wine he had already opened.

Was he really just setting the stage to make it easier for her to embrace his kinky desires?

She told herself not to think that she had anything to do with bringing out this wild and dark creature. But her heart and ego purred like a satisfied kitten, believing only she had this effect on him, believing she had the power to make him cave to his most basic instincts.

She wanted to believe it, but knew how dangerous it was to feel that way. She couldn't let herself feel for him. Especially when she didn't know if his parents would be like Jun's or like Elliot's.

You could ask, she thought, and cursed her brain for it's logical train of thought. She didn't want to know. It would make it harder to walk away from him in six days.

When he came out of the bathroom, he went straight to the refrigerator to retrieve the platter of salami and cheese.

"Want some? I'm going to pop some corn too."

"Sure," she said, knowing he liked to refuel before round two. "Bathroom through there?"

"Yep."

While the popcorn did its thing, Tony sat the platter on a circular end table, and then picked up his remote to turn on *The Empire Strikes Back*. He went back to the kitchen and dug a glass bowl from a cabinet to hold the popcorn. She came out as he was filling their wine glasses.

The smile she gave him was weak, and betrayed the

confident air she was trying to effect. He ushered her over to the couch before she could bolt.

"Take this," he said, handing her the glass of wine. "Relax a little."

Anything but relaxed, she sipped her wine, noted he had turned on her favorite movie.

"What made you turn this on?"

"I saw you watching the first on the plane," he said, pouring the popcorn into his bowl. "It made me want to watch the series."

"I don't like anything after the 90s," she said, wrinkling her nose in response. She perked up when the smell of popcorn hit her after he dropped down next to her.

Tony laughed. "Okay. I get that. Got any plans to go to Star Wars Land?"

"At Disneyland? No. I'd like to, but I just feel like it would be more fun to go with someone. Unfortunately, Gianna and Valerie aren't Star Wars fans. They wouldn't appreciate it."

"I would love to see it. I would love to see a lot of places, actually," he added, scooping up a handful of popcorn. "London, Paris. China."

"You've never been to China?" She gaped at him. "That's just crazy. You have to go."

He lifted his eyebrow. "You've been?"

"Taught English in Beijing for two years."

"Wow," he said, genuinely surprised. He hadn't expected that. "Is that where you learned Chinese?"

"No. I double majored in Spanish and Chinese at UCLA."

"Holy shit. You're trilingual?"

She shrugged. "My Chinese is better, for obvious reasons, but working at DRC has given me more opportunities to speak Spanish. And I've been studying ASL for what feels like forever. It's so hard for me for some reason."

Tony stroked the back of her head. "Probably because you have so many languages in there already."

"Maybe. Why haven't you traveled?"

"The usual excuse. Just didn't have time. My parents had their hands full being in a new city, opening and managing a restaurant, and raising me. Then it was college and working in the restaurant. Now, it's work. Basically, I just never made it a priority."

She realized then that they were slipping into some pretty personal territory and decided to pump the breaks.

"Look," she nodded at the screen. "We're missing it."

He watched the movie, wrapping his arm around her shoulder to pull her close. But just like on the airplane, she couldn't focus with him so close to her. Couldn't focus when she couldn't ignore the fact that this night felt more like a date and less like the string free sex they had agreed to.

They had great chemistry, and the more she got to know him, the more she liked him. And yet, she still didn't feel comfortable letting her guard down. She knew it was unfair, but couldn't seem to stop herself from throwing up a wall between them.

She had to remind him what he had signed up for and reinforce the wall between them.

"What's with the blanket? Part of one of your sexual fantasies?" She asked, sliding her hand across his chest.

Tony pressed his lips to hers when she pulled him toward her. "As a matter of fact, that's exactly why it's there."

"Do tell."

He stroked her lips, watched her with heated eyes. "It involves this pretty little mouth of yours."

She grinned. *Perfect*, she thought, and dropped to her knees.

CHAPTER 9

He was losing her.

Knowing he was, and not knowing what to do about it, made him absolutely miserable. Tony had tried, and failed, over the course of the week to get her to open up to him.

He finagled an invite to her little studio apartment on Wednesday night, and learned that she was a bigger Star Wars fan that he had thought. She had a collection of toys, figurines, and refrigerator magnets throughout the space. When he made the mistake of commenting on it, he saw on her face the moment she realized she had made a mistake letting him in her space. He never got another invite back there.

Saturday came too soon. Every attempt he made to let her know him somehow made her withdraw even further. It frustrated him that she could willingly, even eagerly, give so much to him physically, but give him absolutely nothing emotionally.

He couldn't help wondering if there was something else that he was working against beyond his own stupidity on that first night they met. But when Jun sat him down to lay it all out, he realized that it was much, much worse than anything he could have expected.

Jun pulled off his sweaty t-shirt and tossed it in his

gym bag. "She's going to walk, man. She suspects that you're exactly like her ex, and let's be honest, you were when this thing started."

Tony took a long drink of water to help swallow back the bile that was lodged in his throat. He wanted to tell him, and her, that he was different, that this situation was different.

But the truth of the matter was, he wasn't. Instead of walking away, he pursued her, knowing that his parents wouldn't approve.

"What should I do?" He asked, stuffing his water bottle back inside his bag. "Shit. Is there even any way to fix this?"

"You can tell her the truth," he suggested, pulling on a new shirt.

Tony groaned. "I know. Fuck."

"Maybe she won't walk if she knows your mom is on board."

He shook his head, and then rubbed his hands over his face. "I lied to her. She'll walk. I don't blame her."

"I'm sorry, man."

Tony shrugged, and then hefted his bag over his head. "This whole thing has been fucked from the beginning. Why should it end any differently? I appreciate you telling me, and not kicking my ass too bad in the game."

Jun slapped him on the back. "That was the most pathetic basketball game you've ever played. But I get it. Your head wasn't in the game. But seriously, this conversation never happened. Valerie will kick my ass if she finds out I told you anything about London's ex."

"Valerie may ban me from your house after this shit goes down."

"She's not like that, but Gianna…" Jun trailed off, then shuddered dramatically. "So what are you going to do now?"

"Enjoy my last night with her, and hope she doesn't cut off my balls at the end of it."

∞∞∞∞∞∞∞

Tony left the gym under a cloud of depression, and he was worried it would hang there indefinitely. No matter what she said or did to him once he told her the truth, he hated knowing that under all of the anger, there would be hurt.

Hurt that he could have spared her had he had the strength to stay away from her.

And so tonight, he would do all that he could to take away as much of the sting of pain as possible.

After a quick trip to the barber, he made his way to the Asian market where he picked up the essentials for seafood pan-fried noodles and salt and pepper pork chops.

Having shopped with his parents and prepared these dishes in his father's kitchen as a teen, he chose his ingredients from memory. He decided to round off the meal with some egg rolls from the restaurant. After a quick call to his mother, he stopped by for an uncooked batch.

Tony parked in the rear of the restaurant and sat there a moment, realizing that he felt incredibly reluctant to see his father.

He had always looked up to his father, who had taught him everything about his culture and traditions, about right and wrong, and about hard work and discipline. Tony had always valued those lessons.

It wasn't until high school that he began to look at his father through a different lens. Tony had started working in the kitchen in some capacity at a young age. He washed dishes, mopped floors, and restocked supplies. His first lessons in cooking began when he was twelve.

But because of the child labor laws, he hadn't been allowed to work in the front of the restaurant on the off chance that someone might report his parents for hiring a minor.

In high school, however, he was finally allowed out front. He bussed tables, served food, and took orders. During summer break, his friends or classmates, wanting to see him wait on them, came in what felt like droves.

But all he had really cared about were the girls. His crushes, or those who had crushes on him, often came in after school.

He now knew that his mother had noticed the way he looked at those girls, many of whom were not Chinese. But back then, only his father had made it known that he had seen Tony's ever increasing interest in women of different ethnicities.

And so, at the age of fifteen, his father had sat him down, and promised to disown him if he ever became involved with any girl who wasn't Chinese.

Whenever Tony worked in the restaurant over the next three years, his father would randomly venture out of the kitchen to check on him. When Tony went to pick up plates, he was accused of flirting with the female customers. If he lingered to long taking an order, it was the same thing.

It had been the most exhausting time of his life. As if going through puberty wasn't enough, he had to contend with his father's hyper vigilance. And Tony had easily given in, he realized now. He wanted so badly to please the man who had raised him that he never asked why.

Even now, he didn't know why.

Tony rubbed his hands over his eyes, resentment brewing uncomfortably with the grief that sat in the pit of his stomach. He blamed his father for losing London, though some part of him knew that wasn't fair, he couldn't stop the feeling from taking root.

If his father felt differently about interracial marriage, he wouldn't have to hurt London. He wouldn't lose her.

He wasn't sure how he was going to face the man when he felt that way.

Huan pushed the screen door open and stepped out, shading his eyes as he looked at his son. Realizing he had delayed the inevitable long enough, Tony climbed out of his car and walked across the parking lot.

"What's wrong with you?" Huan asked in spitfire Mandarin.

"I…Nothing, Bà," he responded, not really knowing what else to say. "Just have a lot on my mind."

Huan waved him inside. "Hurry. You'll let in flies."

Tony let the door slam behind him as he stepped inside. Huan moved away quickly to watch over his cooks, always with a critical eye for perfection. There was just a little bit of chaos, and he knew as they moved further into the lunch hour that it would only increase.

He stood and watched for a moment, remembering the little boy who had once admired his father.

Would his father really disown him, he wondered, perhaps for the first time. Would his mother allow it?

It didn't matter, he reminded himself, slipping further into the pit of depression.

London would still leave him, and blaming his father, even changing his mind, wouldn't change that.

"Ma said you're taking a tray of egg rolls. They're in the fridge. Are you having a party?"

"No," he said, walking to the fridge. "They're for a woman I'm seeing."

"Ah, so you really are seeing someone," he mumbled, distracted by one of his cooks. He switched to English, and said, "Plate now. Almost over cook."

Tony turned, surprised. "She told you?"

Huan looked back at him. "Close the door! Your Ma, she's always talking about you and women."

He took the tray out and closed the refrigerator, felt the little seed of hope swell. "What did she say? About the woman I'm seeing."

"All she wants is grandbabies, so I wasn't really listening."

Tony sighed, realizing there was no easy way out of this. "We need to talk. Not today, but soon."

Both of Huan's eyebrows lifted. "So this is a serious relationship then?"

"No," he said, his voice sad. "Not really. We'll talk later, Bà. Maybe next week?"

Huan shrugged, and then turned his attention back to his staff.

Tony carried the tray out to his car, hoping he could shake himself out of this funk before London showed up that night.

A shower helped, but it was cooking that chased away the last dregs of depression. He felt a little more like himself as he prepared the meal.

There was something comforting in the scents that

filled his home, which would probably smell like fried food the next two weeks. It would be the only reminder he had of the one who got away.

London smelled the food in the hallway when she knocked on his door, discovered they were coming from his apartment when he let her in.

"What's all this?" She joined him in the kitchen after she put her purse on the couch. "It's a little late for cooking."

Tony gave her a small smile. "Just felt like cooking, and thought I might share with you."

London broke off a piece of the pan-fried noodle and popped it into her mouth. Simmering in a pan on the stove was a saucy mixture of baby bok choy, carrots, shrimp, and what she assumed was scallops. Egg rolls fried in a pot on the back burner, while pork chops cooled on a plate. She was more than a little impressed.

"You made all of this?"

Now he grinned and handed her a plate. "Don't sound so skeptical. I grew up in my parent's restaurant, and I learned how to cook lots of dishes."

"It's in Sac, yeah? What's it called?" She filled her plate with noodles before pouring a healthy portion of the seafood mix on top.

"New Sun Restaurant."

She turned so quickly to face him that she nearly dropped her plate. Thankfully, he was too busy scooping egg rolls out of the pot to see her staring at him in disbelief.

With her heart all but bursting out of her chest, she set her plate down and eased into the bar stool as her legs began to shake.

"New Sun," she said, clearing her throat when her

voice squeaked a bit. "Is it off Freeport?"

"Yep." Tony turned to place the basket of egg rolls in front of her, and noted that there was a bright look in her eyes. "Sounds like you've been there before."

London bit the inside of her cheek so the grin that would have split her face appeared lopsided. "Ah, yep. It's one of my favorite restaurants."

"Well, hell. I don't know if my cooking will match up to my dad's," he said, making his own plate. "But damn, small world."

Smaller than you think, she thought, grinning madly. "The lady who works the register like a queen on her throne. Is that your mom?"

He grinned because that was such an accurate description. "Yeah, that's her."

"She's really nice. Always gives me extra fortune cookies." She set her chopsticks down, too excited to eat. "And your dad. Mr. Cheng, right? He reminds me of a teddy bear."

Tony set his plate on the bar and blinked at her. "You...you've met my dad?"

"Uh, yeah," she said, wondering why he sounded so shocked. "Why? Is that weird for you?"

"Yes." He laughed, feeling lighter than he had all day. "I mean, no. But, yes, for another reason. He only comes out of the kitchen if there's a problem or..." *Holy shit*, he thought. "Or if he really likes the customer."

London smiled knowingly. "I'm very likeable."

Hope bloomed inside of him. He could make this work. He had to make this work.

"Or you were very naughty." Food forgotten, he came around the island and stood before her. "I'm going to go with naughty."

London stared up at him and gave him her best innocent look. "Me? Naughty? Never!"

"Definitely naughty. I'll have to punish you. Technically, it's my restaurant too. You know, by proxy."

She smirked. "I'm not sure Mrs. Yu would agree."

"Well, I can ask her. But the restaurant keeps them pretty busy. Could be weeks until I can get the full story out of them," he said, pulling her up and wrapping his arms around her waist.

"Mmm. Weeks, huh?"

"At least," he mumbled against her neck.

"Alright," she moaned, dropping her head back as his tongue did delicious things to her neck. "I'll give you four weeks, max, to prove your case."

His heart leapt in his throat. Unable to speak around it, he tightened his grip so he could lift her and carry her to the bedroom.

Her lips sought his, and he poured everything into the kiss, desperate to communicate how much he wanted and needed her. He was shaking with it when he laid her on the bed and covered her body with his own.

But she was desperate to show him everything that she kept locked up inside her for the last two weeks. Like that first night, they tore at each other's clothing, rolling and grappling with each other as they fought to touch, taste, and undress all at the same time. When they were finally naked, she rose up and straddled him.

"Let me," she said.

She didn't give him a chance to argue, but dove for him. She was different, some foggy part of his brain realized as she nipped and sucked on his neck. This was different.

The way her nails raced across his chest, as if she was marking him instead of responding to something he had done to her. As she ventured lower and lower until she took him in her mouth, he realized that this was the first time she was giving him pleasure not as a distraction, but because she wanted to.

The knowledge nearly destroyed him.

"Fuck. London," he squeezed his eyes against the pleasure and pushed up on his elbows. "You have to stop."

She flicked her tongue over him as she spoke. "I guess you better get the condom."

He scooted back on the bed, groaning when her mouth followed, continuing to torture him. With shaky hands, he pulled open the side table drawer and reached in to grab a condom.

He collapsed on the bed and sucked in a startled breath when she sucked one of his balls into her mouth. Cross-eyed, he ripped open the package and rolled the condom on.

Then she straddled him and took him inside. She rocked her hips, riding him slowly, drawing out the pleasure as his hands slid over her thighs. He watched her, his eyes hot and mad with desire, his lips parted as he let out shaky breaths.

And she wanted more, wanted to give him more. He gripped her hips for purchase as she moved faster, dug his nails in her flesh.

Just like the first time, she felt like he was chaining her to him, but this time, she didn't mind. They were already connected, and had been ever since his mother had tried to set them up.

Did he know, she wondered? Did he realize that they had unwittingly been headed toward this moment for almost two years?

She knew now, and rejoiced in the moment. When they came together, she let loose a cry that was part pleasure and part triumph.

She was his, and he was hers, and there was no reason they couldn't be together.

CHAPTER 10

Gianna didn't bother knocking. She shoved the door open, slammed it behind her, and held out her hand for coffee.

Knowing her friend hated getting up early on weekends, London handed her the mug with the coffee prepared exactly as she liked it.

She sipped. Groaned. Then sipped again.

"Okay. Why the hell am I here at eight am? And where's breakfast?"

"About to be gone if you don't get over here," Valerie said around a mouthful of Eggo waffles.

Gianna scowled. "I just bet you've been to the gym and showered already. On a Sunday, no less."

Valerie merely grinned.

"Bitch," she said, fighting back a grin. She sat next to Valerie on the couch, and then pointed to London. "You! Talk. Now!"

"Agreed," Valerie said. "I'm dying to know what's up."

London sat and picked up her mug. "Do you remember that Chinese lady from the restaurant that I told you about? After that whole Yelp fiasco."

"You mean when you trolled that guy until you got him banned from Yelp. Yeah, I remember."

Valerie shook her head and held her hand up. "I am obviously missing a whole hell of a lot. Backstory please."

"Oh, yeah. I forgot. This was before you moved back here. I was at my favorite Chinese restaurant and this guy—"

"White guy," Gianna corrected.

"Yes. He was being a complete dick about the service and the food. He was joking with his friends about getting one of his dishes comped. I started recording him. He demands to see the manager. Mrs. Yu, she comes over and he pretends he can't understand her, makes some racist ass comment about speaking English.

"So I get up and tell him that I've been recording him, and she can use it to sue him for libel. I said I was her lawyer and spoke Chinese to her to add some weight. Then I throw all this legal jargon I've heard them spout in court at him. He's a young guy, so he fell for it. They pay and then head out.

"Mrs. Yu was super grateful, and I guess comfortable enough with me that when I came in a few weeks later, she told me that she suspected those guys were trying to tank their Yelp ratings.

"I checked it out, and based on the dates the reviews were posted, it was pretty clear it was the same guys. So I took a screen shot of some of the reviews and added it with my own review, and the video I took. Reported him to Yelp.

"Any other review he left at any other restaurant I would screenshot his review and warn people not to take his reviews seriously because of what he'd done. Included the link to my Yelp review with the video so people could see it. He eventually got banned."

"Damn, London," Valerie said. "I'm impressed."

London shrugged. "It's not that big of a deal."

"Right. No big deal," Gianna said with a snort. "Didn't you help her refinance their house or something?"

"The loan on the restaurant. I just directed them to a contact I met while working with some clients at DRC. It worked out for them."

"Which is why Mrs. Yu said you should date her son," Gianna provided.

"What?" Valerie sat up, completely surprised. "Damn. What happened with him?"

"Nothing ever happened. She talked about him whenever I came in, but I never met him."

"So you've met him. Is that why we're here? How hot is he? Did you guys hook up? Are you ditching Tony for Mrs. Yu's son?"

"You're here because Tony is Mrs. Yu's son."

She couldn't keep the grin off her face as they gapped at her.

"Tony's mom has been trying to set us up for almost two years. She fricking adores me. And I'm pretty sure his dad does too, despite his tough guy act. This is apparently a big deal. Tony said he only comes out of the kitchen if someone is causing a problem or if it's someone he likes."

"Holy shit!" Gianna set down her mug. "This is some six degrees of separation shit and I am just loving it."

"What did Tony say about his mom trying to hook you two up? How come he never agreed to go out with you?"

"I didn't say anything. Didn't ask. Didn't tell him about his mom. I was just too…"

She trailed off, then leaned back against the couch and heaved a sigh. Valerie sat up and placed a hand on her leg.

"It's okay, London."

"I was happy. I was too happy that my ethnicity isn't going to be the reason we can't be together."

Valerie grinned. "So you guys are together now."

London gave her a satisfied smile. "We agreed to keep seeing each other."

"Tony and London sitting in the tree! K-I-S-S-I-N-G!"

London laughed. "You're ridiculous."

Gianna grinned. "Seriously. What's next? Are you going to tell him?"

"Eventually. Right now, I just want to enjoy him with the full knowledge that there is no reason that we can't be together."

"I wonder how he'll react when he finds out you two could have been dating years ago," Valerie said.

"And why he didn't listen to his mom," Gianna added.

"If my mom tried to set me up with someone, I wouldn't listen either."

"Yeah, I guess you're right," Gianna grinned. "I'm really happy for you, London."

"Not mad at me for waking you up so early?"

Gianna filled her plate with more waffles.

"I am, and will be until you tell me the rest."

London looked at her in confusion. "The rest?"

"The rest. I'm not getting laid, remember? I'm betting the sex was off the charts hot after all that came out. I'm going to need some deets with these waffles."

London laughed until her sides hurt, and then gave her all the deets.

∞∞∞∞∞∞

His parent's restaurant was closed to the public on Mondays, but he knew they would be inside.

His father would be overseeing the kitchen's weekly deep cleaning while simultaneously checking his stock and supplies for the order he would place at the end of the day. Since he still wasn't ready to talk to him, Tony decided it best to enter through the front instead of the kitchen.

He wanted confirmation before he had that talk with his dad. If London was in fact the woman his mother had tried to set him up with in the past, then the conversation might go differently. It might not go as bad as he had originally assumed it would.

He was certain that if anyone had the charm and heart to win over his parents, it would be London. But he wanted to be sure.

Using his key, he unlocked the front door and let himself in. The cleaners had already finished here, so the floors and tables gleamed and the sweet scent of the chemicals filled the air.

Mei paused from counting plates. "Tony. What are you doing here?"

"I know you're busy, so I'll make this quick. I need to know about the black woman you were trying to set me up with. What's her name?"

"London. Did things not work out with the other woman?"

The breath that he hadn't realized that he had been holding whooshed out of him, making him a little light headed. He sat in the nearest chair.

"I'm an idiot. I wasted so much time."

"What are you talking about?" Mei asked, coming to his side in concern, and confusion.

Tony shifted and pulled his phone from his pocket. Unlocking it, he pulled open his photos and found one of the wedding party.

"This is the woman I'm seeing. A few nights ago, we learned that my parents own her favorite restaurant."

Mei walked over, her face scrunched up as she tried to make sense of the photo. She saw Jun and the lovely bride she had seen the other day. Then she saw Tony and the woman next to him. She leaned down, looking harder, before her face brightened.

"London? You're seeing London?"

"She's best friend's with Jun's bride. I met her in February, but we didn't start dating until the wedding."

"You should listen to your mother."

Tony gave her a weak smile. "Yeah, I see that now."

"You're worried about Bà," she said solemnly and moved to sit beside him.

He sighed. "She said he likes her, but will he accept our relationship? I'll lose her if he doesn't. I'll lose Bà if I choose her."

Mei said nothing at first. She trusted her husband to make the right decision, but men were emotional creatures. It might take him weeks or months to get there. She knew that wasn't what Tony wanted to hear.

"I'll talk to him today. When I think he's ready to talk, I'll have you both come over."

"Thank you, Ma."

"It might take time, Tony. Be patient."

Tony nodded and rose from the table. He gave his mother a hug before leaving the restaurant, locking up behind him. Inside of his car, he stared out the window.

Time felt like his enemy right now. It was like he was holding a balloon and each day he didn't tell the full truth, time made it bigger and bigger. It was going to explode. He could only hope that they survived the blast.

∞∞∞∞∞∞

"I'm just saying. If you're introducing me to your friends, I think that bumps this thing up a bit and warrants six weeks instead or four."

"Pushing your luck. I may hate you in six weeks."

Tony waited until he came to a complete stop before he looked over at her with all the skepticism he could muster.

"You never know," she said, trying not to grin.

"Sounds like I need to spend the night reminding you why that will never happen. Let's just skip this whole thing and head back right now."

"Light's green."

He went back to hunting for a parking space in Oak Park. They were meeting London's friend at the popular summer event called Gather to eat, drink, and be merry with people from all walks of life in the Sacramento community.

It was a free event designed to celebrate everything that Sacramento represented, and had been a complete success thus far.

He had heard about it, but as he preferred to enjoy the June heat from the inside of his air-conditioned apartment, he had yet to experience it.

"How's this spot? Going to have to walk a little, but this seems like the best we can do."

"Sure, that works."

He parked, and then climbed out of the car. Even at seven pm, the summer heat was like a punch to the face. Still, he took her hand as they walked down the street, enjoying the contact, as always.

Oak Park, established in 1973, was a neighborhood in Sacramento that was experiencing revitalization or gentrification, depending on which side of the line you stood. As such, the buildings that lined the street were a mixture of both old and new.

Gather Oak Park took the streets between Broadway and 3rd Avenue and transformed them into a giant living and dining space. Blocks away, he could already feel the base from the live band and smell the scents of various food trucks and vendors.

"We've been seeing each other for almost six weeks now. I vote, especially because of the friend thing, that we revisit in six weeks instead of four."

London smiled over at him. "You're cute when you beg."

When they stopped at the cross walk, he pulled her to him, bit her lip.

"And you're fucking hot when I make you beg."

"Don't change the subject," she said, rubbing her lips against his before stepping back. "If tonight goes well, I will consider giving this thing another six weeks."

"It will go well."

Tony pulled her across the street after the light changed. Things had been going well, and he was beginning to feel confident that they would continue to do so.

Ever since she found out that she knew and liked his parents, he noticed that she began to take down the wall that she had built between them. It allowed him to pursue her, and their relationship, as if they were actually in one.

In the last four weeks, he took her to the movies and to dinner. Instead of rolling in, bouncing on him, and rolling out when they were through, she stayed the night most weekends. And now he was meeting one of her friends and coworkers.

He knew, though he forced that bit of logic as far back in the recesses of his mind as he could, that she was under the impression that both of his parents were on board with interracial dating.

He knew he should have told the truth and corrected her, laid it all out and given her the choice to stay or leave. But since he was sure that unless she loved him that she would leave him, he kept it from her.

It was the hardest thing he had ever done.

At the entrance, they showed their IDs and received a wristband so they could purchase alcohol without getting carded each time. As they moved past the barriers and into the heart of the event, the crowds swallowed them up.

They agreed to wander first in order to get a feel for what their options were in terms of food and alcohol. When they decided on what they wanted, they divided and conquered.

London looked over the menu as her foot tapped to the beat of the music. The upbeat rhythm only added to her mood, making the joy she felt inside form on her lips.

It had been an amazing four weeks. Easy, she thought. It was so easy to be with him. They joked and teased about their no strings sex pact ending, but deep down, she thought they both knew that what they had was more than that.

Still, playing the game was just another of the many interesting aspects of their relationship. And she rather liked it when he made her beg.

After she ordered their food, she moved to the side to get a better view of the band. She wondered if he would keep playing the game or risk making it official. There was so little she held back from him now, so he had to know that she was as bought in as he was.

Assuming that he was. Before she could explore that train of thought, a familiar face moved into her line of sight.

"Daydreaming as usual, I see."

"Some things never change I guess," she said.

Elliot grinned. "You look great, London. How have you been?"

"Good. Really good, actually," she added, smiling genuinely as she recalled her earlier thoughts about Tony. "How have you been?"

"Okay," he said, a cautious smile on his lips. He moved in closer to her. "Can we go somewhere and talk?"

"No," she said. That he asked meant it was long past time to get this over with. "I thought about it like you asked, and the answer is no."

His face fell. "London, please."

"Elliot," she said with a sigh. "No."

"How about one date? Just to see if we've still got some heat. Come on, London. I'm willing to walk away from my family for you."

Her eyes went flat. "That. That right there is why we will never happen. The resentment is already there, ready to take root and bloom the moment something doesn't go your way. You'll hold the fact that you chose me instead of listening to your parents over my head for as long as it suits you."

Her name was called and she moved away from him to grab her food. He followed after her.

"You need to let go and move on, Elliot. I already have and that's the other reason this wouldn't work."

She turned and found Tony standing there. The look he sent Elliot was far from friendly.

"Good timing. I just got our food. Let's go find a seat. I'm starving."

Since she didn't spare the Asian guy another look, Tony thought he should do the same. He didn't need to add any fuel to the jealous rage that was currently burning in his gut.

He didn't know what had been said, but he recognized the look on that man's face. He wanted London, and he hadn't been afraid to make it known.

If that guy was trying to move in on his woman, he would have to set him straight.

"Was that guy bothering you?" He shouted, following closely behind her.

"Not more than usual. Here!"

A couple left their seats and London quickly slid in to replace them, setting her food on the communal table as she did. There were about six tables lined up together down the street, forcing, and encouraging attendants to gather together to break bread.

"Smells great. I think I made a good choice."

Tony slid her drink in front of her. "So you knew that guy?"

"Yes. Don't worry about him. I don't."

He wanted to push and pry, but since he worried her answer would lead him to commit murder, he let it go.

Her phone rang and she quickly picked it up. "We're in the middle I think, at the tables. We're closer to the entrance."

Tony wondered where this nervous feeling had come from as he listened to her relay directions to her friend. When they finally showed up, he told himself to relax. He knew she was joking about the six weeks, but it somehow felt tremendously important to make a good impression on anyone who was in her life.

He stood and shook hands. "Nice to meet you guys. Do you want to sit?"

Iris shook her head. "I'm fine. You sit and eat. I'm entirely too excited to sit still anymore."

Evan grinned over at her. "I'm amazed you've kept it in this long. Spit it out already."

London stopped eating and looked closely at Iris. Her eyes were brighter than usually.

"What? What is it?"

"We bought a house!" She squealed.

"What! Oh my gosh! Congrats! I didn't realize you put in an offer on anything."

"She didn't want to jinx it," Evan shared. "It's been so hard for us to agree on something or not get outbid, so we kept it quiet."

"This is so exciting! Tell me everything!"

While Tony and London ate, Iris shared all the details. Tony could see that while Iris was all excited energy, Evan stood beside her like a mountain. He radiated calm, but he could see the love and affection for Iris in the man's eyes. They seemed to perfectly balance each other. He wondered if people would say that about him and London.

"Wow. 15 day close. For people who aren't Iris, that

would be difficult. You hang in there, Evan."

Evan laughed. "You know my girl well, London. I'll survive somehow. If you can convince her not to have a house warming on the Fourth of July, I'd appreciate it."

London gaped at Iris. "Eight days after you move in? Are you insane?"

"Absolutely," she said with a wink.

London laughed. "I'll help in whatever way I can."

They walked around, continuing to shout at each other over the noise. They drank more beer and stood amongst the crowds on the edge of the dance floor, swaying to the music.

When it was time for them to leave, London and Tony said their goodbyes. As they walked out, Tony felt a weird itch between his shoulder blades. He glanced back and saw Evan talking to the guy London had been with at the food truck. The guy was staring at London with a look of longing.

Tony turned away and tried to ignore the burning in his gut. He wondered what happened between that man and London, if only so he didn't repeat whatever mistake he had made.

CHAPTER 11

London arrived at Iris' new place at twelve pm on the Fourth of July. As she climbed from the car, the heat immediately enveloped her and the sun just about blinded her eyes. Sacramento summers often meant it was ninety degrees by noon, and this day had definitely delivered.

Leave it to Iris to throw a house warming party on the hottest day of the month. She wouldn't say that it was the hottest day of the year since they still had to get through August. And, if she was being honest, it was entirely too early to be calling today the hottest day of the month.

Chuckling to herself, she retrieved her bag with her change of clothes from the seat and tossed it over her shoulder. Amused by her weather observations, she thanked the ride share driver and closed the door. She generally didn't complain about the summer heat since it wouldn't change a thing.

Iris and Evan's new condo was nestled next to a man-made lake in Elk Grove. She caught glimpses of the picturesque gated community on the drive in and thought it suited her friends perfectly.

Iris stood waiting for her in the doorway. "Hello and welcome!"

London grinned as she approached. "Don't be so excited to put me to work."

"There's not that much to do, I swear."

London kicked off her sandals at the doorstep. "I believe you. I would still be unpacking if I had moved in eight days ago."

She stepped into a small tiled entryway at the base of the stairway. She followed Iris up, enjoying the quick tour of the two bedroom, two bath home.

The galley style kitchen was wide enough for at least three people to move comfortably around in. Both the cabinets and countertops were white. It was an excellent contrast to the dark toned laminate flooring throughout. Stainless steel appliances gleamed as if they had been freshly polished.

A small dining space was next to the kitchen and had a black bar height dining table that seated four. Beyond that was a spacious living room where a gray loveseat and sofa faced the large window.

"It's like dual masters," London pointed out after the tour was complete.

"Yep," Iris agreed. "It's one of the reasons why we went with this one. Figured that would work in our favor when it's time to sell."

"Always thinking ahead," London said, moving back into the dining room. "It looks great. I can't believe how big the living room is. And the kitchen is the perfect size."

"Thanks. I really love it here."

"So what do you need me to do? We have an hour and half before people start showing up and I want to change before they get here."

"Let's get the decorations up, and then I'll have you handle the second bath. I haven't put out my nice towels and all that yet, and it probably should be cleaned again. While you do that, I'll get the kitchen ready for when Elliot gets here with the food."

Her stomach dropped. "Damn. Really?"

Iris scowled. "Trust me, I was pretty miffed when I found out. Of all the people who could have helped."

London sighed and took the bag of decorations Iris passed her. "I wouldn't be surprised if Elliot insisted on picking up the food just so he could get over here early."

"He's out of his mind for thinking that you would get back with him."

"Completely. I know I haven't done anything in the last two years that would make him think I was still interested in him."

Iris climbed on the couch to hang the banner. "I've seen you have friendlier conversations with perfect strangers."

"I'm not even sure how I'll be around him now that I know that he wants me back."

"Won't Tony be here?"

"Yes. That just makes it more awkward. I don't know why I thought I could handle being in the same room as my ex and my…my boyfriend, I guess."

Iris laughed. "You've been seeing him since April. I think boyfriend is accurate."

London twirled a streamer in her hand. "We haven't talked about labels, but I would agree."

"How do you feel about that?" Iris asked as she sat on the couch. "How do you think he'll feel about that?"

"I think he'd be okay with it too. I know that I've basically been on cloud nine since I found out about his parents," she confessed with a goofy grin.

"Does he know about Elliot?"

London sighed. "You know I hate to rehash all of that drama."

"Oh, I know." Iris pushed off the couch and moved into the kitchen. "I can barely believe that you've kept Valerie and Gianna in the dark about him still being around."

London shrugged. "What difference does it make? It doesn't change what happened, or the fact that he'll be around."

Iris set about opening a bottle of wine. "I guess. But if you keep coming around Evan and I while you're with Tony, he's bound to pick up on something when Elliot's around."

"You're probably right. Don't give me that smug look," London scowled. She accepted the glass of wine. "I'll tell him. Sooner rather than later."

As she walked to the bathroom, London wondered how she would broach that subject. She didn't like to talk about Elliot. Breakups inevitably happened. She often wondered if her friends simplified her feelings around their falling out to something akin to embarrassment. It wasn't that simple for her.

London frowned at her reflection in the mirror. Truth be told, she didn't like talking about Elliot because she had to talk about racism and stereotypes. It made her deeply uncomfortable to acknowledge that she had been treated unfairly because of something she had no way of changing.

If she made a mistake or if someone just didn't like her personality, then that outcome, whatever it was, would have been easier to deal with than being forced to acknowledge that the color of her skin was the root cause.

It was much, much more comfortable, and probably a little unhealthy, to move through the world with blinders so that she didn't see all of the bigotry, racism, stereotyping and other micro aggressions.

Living in the diverse city of Sacramento afforded her privilege of a much more comfortable life as a black person in America. Perhaps that's why it was so much harder to talk about things that happened to her.

London sighed as she wiped down the counter, already dreading the conversation. Tony had already noticed the tension between her and Elliot at Gather, so at the very least she would tell him that Elliot was her ex. He didn't need to know the full story.

Feeling a little better, London arranged candles and seashells on the counter. When she was done, she hung the new shower curtain and set the mats on the floor. She came out of the bathroom just as Elliot walked up the stairs.

He stopped short when he saw her, staring at her intently before he moved into the kitchen. He was already dressed for the party in a crisp white tank with the American flag sitting on the center of his chest and blue shorts.

"Thanks, Elliot. Can you bring up the drinks and cooler from the garage? Appreciate it. London, let's get this set up."

London had to hide her smile when she heard the rapid-fire orders. Elliot looked at her again before he disappeared downstairs. The next half hour went by much like that. Iris did her best to keep them separate as they finished setting up for the party.

Ten minutes before the guests were due to arrive, Iris pulled London into her bedroom and shut the door so they could change.

London tossed her bag on the bed. "I fucking love you."

Iris pulled her shirt over her head. "I'd prefer to be thanked for slapping him, but since I can't slap him, I'll accept that instead."

"Such is life," she said, pulling off her own clothes.

"You're absolutely right and I'm allowed to be mad about that."

It took them longer than ten minutes to get dressed, and by the time they came out of the bedroom, a few guests had already arrived. While Iris played hostess, London poured herself another glass of wine and made a small plate of food.

It amused her to be eating Chinese food in room with red, white, and blue party decorations. Since the party would be over before nightfall, Iris assumed all of them would go to another party where they would find the more traditional Fourth of July food. She appreciated the consideration because as much as she loved BBQ hot dogs and hamburgers, she didn't want to eat them at every party she went to that day.

London sat at the table and saw Elliot move into the kitchen and quickly grab a plate. She sincerely hoped he wasn't going to try to talk to her here, but the way he kept stealing glances at her quickly dashed that hope to bits. Just as he was trying to make his way around the other people who had joined him in the kitchen, Tony appeared at the top of the stairs.

She bolted up from the table and took his hand. "Hi."

"Hi." He kissed her before letting her pull him to the table. "Save some for me?"

"Of course," she said, offering him a bite of food. "Eat up and then we can mingle."

And so they ate and drank and mingled. Eventually, she forgot all about Elliot. But Tony was aware of him, and couldn't relax as a result. He kept looking at London. Looking at them as if he was just waiting for an opening so he could talk to her.

It occurred to him that London had introduced him to everyone at the party except for the man that kept staring at her. There was definitely something between them, even though it appeared to be one sided. Still, it was obvious that she didn't want to acknowledge whatever the hell that was.

He wanted to know. Moreover, he couldn't shake the feeling that it was vitally important that he knew who that man was to her.

"All right everyone," Evan announced, interrupting Tony's thoughts. "I know some of you may start heading out to your next destination soon, so we wanted to make sure we thanked everyone for stopping by."

Iris grinned at him. "My guy. So proper."

Evan grinned in return. "I'm glad you said that because…"

Gasps echoed around the room as Evan dropped to one knee in front of Iris. As Iris squealed in disbelief, Evan pulled the ring from his pocket.

"Let's keep things proper, even if it's out of the traditional order. Will you marry me?"

"Oh my gosh. I can't believe you did this! Yes, of course. Oh my gosh. Look at it!"

The room erupted in noise. Shouts, cheers, whistling and sounds of sniffling could be heard as everyone congratulated the couple. Beside him, London shed more than a few tears. Thankfully, someone was already passing around tissue.

He kissed her cheek. "Go congratulate your friend."

London rose to do just that. They spent the next hour gushing over her ring and laughing at everything Evan had to go through to keep Iris from finding out about and interfering with his plan to propose.

As guests began to disappear, London remembered that they had their own plans.

"We should get going," she said to Tony. Then rose to embrace Iris. "I'm so happy for you two."

"Don't make me start crying again," Iris pleaded.

"Better now than at the wedding," London joked.

Iris laughed. "Thank you. I needed that. I'll see you two later."

"Congrats," Tony said. "Thanks for the invite."

They headed down and at the bottom of the stairs, London realized she forgot her bag. She ran back up to get it while Tony went out to get his car. When she made her way downstairs again, Elliot followed.

"We need to talk," he demanded.

"No, we don't."

"London, please—"

London pulled her hand away when he tried to grab it. "Elliot, enough."

He jumped in front of her to block her path to the driveway. "I just want a chance to explain."

"It's not going to change anything!" She shouted. "We broke up two years ago. What we had is over."

"So let's start over," he pleaded.

"Seriously?" She gaped at him in confused irritation. "Did you not see my boyfriend upstairs?"

"You've known me for two years. That guy is a stranger by comparison. His parents aren't going to allow their son to be with a black woman, and you don't know if he's willing to choose you over them.

You know it with me.”

Stunned by his boldness, she took a step back. “Wow.”

“Look,” he took her hand when she started to move past him. “I'm not trying to be hurtful, but that is why some Asian men don't date black women. It's not a factor for me anymore. I want you, and I want to make this work, no matter what my parents say.”

“What the hell? Get your hands off her.”

They both looked over as Tony burst from his car and strode over to them.

“Let go of me, Elliot,” she said, her voice low and flat.

“London—”

“She said let go,” Tony growled, taking her hand to tug her behind him. “Keep your hands off of her. Better yet, stay the hell away from her.”

“Yeah, I don't think so,” Elliot chuckled darkly, leaning closer to Tony. “I'll be right here when you screw up. You may have her fooled, but I see it. You're just like me. Scared shitless.”

“You need to back the fuck up,” he demanded.

“You're scared all right. Scared she's going to leave you when she finds out your parents don't approve of your relationship with her.” Elliot stepped to the side to look at London. “Whatever he's told you about his parents, it's a lie.”

“Look—” Tony began.

“That's enough, Elliot,” she interrupted. “Whatever you were hoping would happen between us, you need to let it go.” She met his eyes and hoped he saw the truth. “I don't feel anything for you anymore, and I never will. What little I felt for you died the day we broke up.”

She turned away and walked to the car. Tony sent Elliot a look of disgust before jogging to catch up with her. He opened the door for her and closed it when she was in.

As he rounded the hood, Elliot shouted, "You're going to be me."

Tony flipped him off, but inside, his stomach tied in knots. He knew now that Elliot was the ex boyfriend that Jun had told him about. The ex boyfriend who had only been interested in London for the sex since his parents wouldn't approve of him being with a black woman.

The ex boyfriend who London had assumed Tony was like when he didn't immediately pursue her. And he was like her ex a lot more than he was comfortable to admit.

Tony stared straight ahead as he drove, afraid to look at her. Afraid that she might see the fear that Elliot had seen.

"Let's get you home, okay?"

"No. Let's go to Valerie's. He means too little to me to let him spoil our plans."

He forced a smile and looked over at her. "Okay."

She smiled in return, and for the rest of the night, they both pretended that everything was okay.

∞∞∞∞∞∞

"I should explain," she said quietly when they exited his car a few hours later.

Tony glanced over at her. They had done their best at their friend's house, but the altercation with Elliot hung like a heavy cloud over them the whole night and made it difficult for them to truly relax and enjoy.

"You don't have to explain," he responded. "It's obvious that your ex is still crazy for you and I can't blame him. He was stupid to let you go."

The words felt heavy on his heart. Elliot wasn't the only stupid one and since he knew it, he felt like a complete fraud for trying to comfort her.

"He didn't feel like he had a choice. His parents…" She began hesitantly. "His parents want him to be with a Korean woman. Not only was a black woman out of the question, he gave me the impression that they don't even like black people."

Tony pulled her into a hug after they entered the elevator. He didn't know what to say. He was no stranger to racism, but it never felt good to confront it. And now he wondered if his own father felt that way about black people. If racism was the reason he threatened to disown him if he didn't marry a Chinese woman.

This was worse, much worse, than what Jun had told him.

"I know that discrimination and racism are awful, but I wouldn't wish for anyone to be estranged from their family. And being the cause of it?" She shook her head as she followed him down the hallway. "I would never forgive myself."

"It wouldn't have been your fault, London," he said, unlocking his door. "Elliot and his parents made their choice and any consequences are on them."

He needed this to stop. The more she told him, the worse his own omission made him feel. He closed the door behind them and pulled her into his arms. Hoping to distract her, he walked her backward inside as he nuzzled her neck with his nose. Her head tilted to the side and she placed her hands on his elbows for balance. But he wasn't in the clear just yet.

"I…when you didn't ask me out," she said, stumbling over the words when he began nibbling on her earlobe. "I thought that your parents were just like his. I thought you were just like him."

He wanted to tell her to stop. He had to make her stop so he lifted her up and over his shoulder. He slapped her ass and carried her to his room.

"I'm nothing like him," he lied. *I'm exactly like him.*

Tony dropped her on the bed. She scooted back and lay down. When she looked up at him with hooded eyes full of desire, he had to fight the urge to beg for her forgiveness.

"Show me."

He covered her body with his. Covered her mouth with his own. Could she taste his desperation? His fear? He hoped not. He wanted to show her the love that was in his heart.

Fuck it all. He needed to show her that he was in love with her.

Tony ordered his hands and mind to be gentle, to go slow. He had to show her now and every chance he got how much he loved her. He braced himself on one elbow and cupped the back of her neck with his other.

Slowly, softly, his pressed his lips to hers before brushing them over her cheek.

"You're so beautiful," he whispered.

He kissed her again, gentle and slow, coaxing out a small sigh of pleasure, of surrender. He moved to her neck, taking his time there as his hand moved down to inch it's way under her shirt. Shifting his weight down, he leaned over to place soft kisses from her navel to her breast.

London's body arched up off the bed in offering as

much as pleasure. "Show me. All of you."

Tony stopped and looked up at her, guessing what she meant. "Are you sure?"

"Yes," she said, meeting his eyes.

He shouldn't. He shouldn't because he didn't deserve the trust he was about to ask of her. He had hinted at some of his darker desires a handful of times, but had only acted on what he considered to be the tamest. He shouldn't show her more, but he couldn't deny her. He would wait to show her all when he had the right to.

He pushed off of her and leaned over to open the bottom drawer of his nightstand. He rummaged around until he found the small silk bag. If he couldn't tie her to him, tying her to his bed was the next best thing.

London's heart raced in anticipation when he pulled her up. She thought that he kissed her in order to distract her, but she couldn't stop looking at the small bag even as he pulled her shirt over her head. He brushed his fingertips over her shoulders when he pushed her bra straps down. She reached up automatically to unclasp her bra, her eyes glued to the bag.

"Lay back," he whispered in Mandarin. "Put your arms above your head."

She did as he asked and bit her tongue when he used the satin scarves inside the bag to tie her hands to his metal headboard. When his eyes passed over her, she thought she might burn from the heat that she saw in them.

"You're mine," he said, his voice dark with pleasure. He unsnapped her shorts and started tugging them and her panties down her legs.

"Yes," she whispered.

He tied her feet to the footboard. She felt vulnerable while he leaned back to survey her naked body. Nervous, she tugged at the scarves to test their strength.

"I wondered why you had a bed with a bar on the footboard and headboard."

Tony stood to undress. "Just say stop if it's too much."

London let out a nervous breath. "What are you going to do?"

"You're mine. I'm going to make sure every inch of you knows it."

He started with her neck and moved down her body. Systematically, gleefully, and painstakingly claimed her. Nipping, biting, sucking, pinching, squeezing, and scratching every inch of her body as promised. There was fleeting pain and intense pleasure. The whirlwind of it made her head spin and still she wanted more. She gasped and cried out, bucked and tugged at the restraints enough to loosen them.

He growled in response, and the dark joy that filled her heart when he pinned both of her hands above her head with one of his own shocked her. Then his other hand moved between her legs and played with her until the orgasm shattered her to pieces.

Reeling from it, she was barely aware that Tony was tying both of her hands together over her head. He moved off of her, leaving her body cold and yearning for his warmth. She whimpered when she heard him open the condom and wondered if she should tell him to stop. But the moment his body touched hers and he slipped inside her, she thought of nothing but him. Wanted nothing but him.

He hooked an arm under each of her legs, filling her deeper. Hard and steady, he moved inside of her until he felt his whole body begin to fall apart. Their eyes locked, held.

"You're mine. Every inch of you."

"Yours. Every inch," she said.

As they came together, her heart leapt out of her chest and into his hands.

CHAPTER 12

He couldn't sleep.

Tony held London tightly against him, the guilt eating at him as he listened to her quiet breathing. He knew he should tell her the truth about everything. The real reason he didn't pursue her that first night. His father's promise to disown him.

The longer that he kept the truth from her, the more damage it would do to their relationship when it all came out. He would be lucky if they still had a relationship after.

Maybe he could prevent it from being a complete disaster. He just needed to hash things out with his dad. Hopefully his mom had made some progress on convincing his dad not to disown Tony for not being with a Chinese woman. At this point, he would take him being open to the conversation around it.

Regardless of where his father stood, he couldn't put that conversation off any longer.

Letting London believe that both his parents were on board with their relationship wasn't a lie that he felt he could keep telling now that he knew that he loved her. He had to do whatever he could to keep her, and being honest with her was something he had to do.

At sunrise, he gave up on trying to sleep. He slipped

from the bed and pulled on his clothes from the day before. After checking that his wallet and keys were still in his pockets, he headed out of the apartment.

The coffee shop was just unlocking its doors when he walked up. Once he had his coffee, he sat and gave himself exactly two minutes to stall before he picked up the phone to call his dad.

"What happened?" His father demanded to know, his voice gruff with sleep.

"Nothing. I'm fine. I need to talk to you. Today."

Huan was silent for a moment. "Sounds important."

"It is," he said.

"It's Friday, and the restaurant might be busier today because of the holiday."

"Can you meet me there at nine? I can help prep while we talk."

Huan grunted. "Okay."

"Okay," Tony said with an audible exhale. "See you then."

He hung up and pressed his hand to his heart. It was racing. He felt hot, and he didn't attribute it to the coffee. He wasn't ready for this conversation. He wasn't ready for the outcome.

If his father didn't sway, he could be disowned. Or, worse, much worse, he realized as sweat dotted his brow, he could lose the woman he loved if she wasn't willing to let him walk away from his family.

Tony wiped the sweat from his forehead with the back of his hand before rising to order another coffee for himself and one for London. While he waited for his order, he tried to find calm. If he went back to his apartment acting like the basket case that he felt like, she would suspect something was wrong.

She would ask him what was wrong in her gentle,

caring way and he would completely break down and tell her everything before he had a chance to speak with his father.

So he forced himself to think positive thoughts as he walked back to his apartment. This would work. This had to work. He couldn't lose her.

The apartment was quiet when he let himself in, making him think that she wasn't awake yet. But he heard the sound of the shower as soon as he stepped inside his room. He placed her cup on the counter.

"Tony?" She called.

"Yeah. I'm back."

London turned off the water and pulled a towel inside to dry off. "Where did you go?"

"I missed a call from my dad last night, so I called him back. Somebody called out so I need to go in and give him a hand."

"July fifth should be a federal holiday. It's hard to go back to work after a day of eating and drinking and a night of fireworks."

"Since it isn't, I had to go get a good, strong cup of coffee. Brought your usual."

She stepped out of the shower, expecting him to be there. Instead, the coffee sat on the counter and she saw him walking back to his room. He opened his closet and pulled out a shirt.

"Does that mean you have to go soon?" She asked, the pout evident in her voice.

"We have a little more time left," he said quietly before he turned to her.

Wrapped in the towel, London approached him. "Why the long face?"

"I…" He reached out to touch her face, watching her intently. "I didn't freak you out last night, did I?"

London stepped up to him so that their bodies touched. "I'm still here, aren't I?"

"Yeah," he said with a heavy sigh.

She rose up on his toes to give him a chaste kiss. "Is that why you snuck out of bed? You were worried that I would be freaked out?"

He bit his lip. "I did tie you to the bed."

"And yet, I can't help but think you still held back. There's more in there that you're hiding, isn't there?"

He gave an audible gulp because she had no idea. "We'll have time for that. You're mine, right?"

She grinned. "Right."

"Good," he said, forcing himself to smile. "I'm going to go shower. You go relax. Enjoy your day off."

She rolled her eyes when he walked away. She was entirely too energized to relax. He was lucky that she didn't join him in that shower and do something deliciously inappropriate to burn off the energy.

She was in love with him and she had every confidence that one day he would be in love with her.

For the first time in what felt like forever, she was in a healthy relationship. She couldn't stop smiling about it. It might be happening too fast, but she had never felt such a deep connection before. They simply balanced each other and fit.

A feeling like this called for pancakes. Surely he had time for pancakes before he had to be at the restaurant. They would have breakfast together and then he could drop her off at her place.

Since she had forgotten her bag in his car, she rummaged through his dresser for a t-shirt and a pair of basketballs shorts. Dressed, she went to the kitchen and pulled out what she needed.

As she worked, she decided she would drop by his

parent's restaurant later that day. It had been a while since she had brought Mr. Cheng a pie, and she hadn't talked to Mrs. Yu for some time either.

Tony would likely be there through the lunch rush. If she timed it well, she could have lunch with him and his mom. Maybe his dad would come out and join them.

Satisfied with her plan, she started on her first pancake with a happy smile on her face.

∞∞∞∞∞∞

Tony unlocked the back door of the restaurant. Since he hadn't seen his father's car, he was prepared for the warning beeps from the alarm system, promising to sound if not disabled. He went straight to the panel to disarm it before he turned on the lights. After slipping his keys in his pocket, he looked around, reminiscing.

He had spent so much of his childhood back here. In the eerie stillness and quiet, like it was now, to the chaotic and organized whirlwind of the dinner rush. He remembered the cadence of his father's steady voice when he let him cook on the big stove for the first time. How his hand, heavy and comforting, had gently corrected his movements.

They had sat together at the small table at the back corner going over menus and budgets and paperwork for the restaurant. Even when he began to make his own suggestions, to argue for them, he and his father always got along.

It seemed, Tony realized, that the only point of contention between them was whom he could date.

Tony began putting dishes away and wondered, not

for the first time, why his father was so adamant about him being with a Chinese woman. He never questioned it, even when he wanted to. Maybe if he had, they wouldn't be where they were today.

His entire body tensed when he heard the backdoor open. Even now, he didn't want to have this conversation. But he knew he had to.

Huan hadn't bothered to shave that morning so the stubble that dotted his chin was black and white. For some reason, it made his frown that much more prominent. He wore a black t-shirt and green shorts, which he quickly covered with a black apron. He stared at Tony as he tied it on.

"I assume this is about the woman your mom has been nagging me about." His frown deepened. "The black woman."

Tony's jaw clenched. "Yes, this is about London."

Huan blinked. "You're seeing London? The black woman who speaks Mandarin?"

"Yes," Tony replied. He had assumed his mother had told his father everything, but she had obviously left some things out. "We've been together since April."

Huan frowned again. The new information bothered him, and he wasn't exactly sure why. Needing a moment to process it, he went to the pantry to haul out the bucket of rice. When he returned, Tony was filling the rice bowl with water.

"Still ten cups in each?"

Huan nodded and passed Tony the bucket of rice. While Tony started to wash the rice, Huan retrieved the clipboard he used to take stock of his inventory. His jaw ticked as he did. He couldn't focus.

"Why couldn't you choose a Chinese woman?"

There was a tense moment of silence before Tony turned around to face his father.

"Why do I have to be with a Chinese woman?"

"You know why!" Huan glared at him. "I told you so many times."

"Yeah, I remember." Tony gritted his teeth, fighting back the anger. "I remember every single time you threatened to disown me if I looked at girl who wasn't Chinese. I'm asking you why. What's your reasoning? There has to be another reason other than because you said so."

"Because it makes sense. You would have the same customs and traditions, the same views on the importance and value of family. These Americans, they only value their money and their independence. You will lose everything I taught you, everything that makes you Chinese by being with an American woman."

A little sliver of hope wormed its way through the cloud of fear and anger clouding Tony's mind.

"And that's your hang up? The fact that she's American, not that she's..." he trailed off, hoping it wasn't the reason. "Not because she's black."

Huan turned red with indignation. "I only care that she's not Chinese. I don't care that she speaks Mandarin, or that she lived in China. It's not the same. If you pursue this relationship with her..."

He trailed off, letting the threat hang there. Tony wondered why he couldn't say the words now when they had rolled off his tongue so easily in the past.

"How do you know that she doesn't have similar values? Why do you assume that she would ask me to throw away my customs and traditions to be with her? Better yet, how do you know that the Chinese woman you envision me being with would have the same customs and traditions as we do? What if she's just as American as London is?"

When Huan didn't respond, Tony continued.

"You don't know. Deep down, you know that being Chinese doesn't mean we're all the same and therefore perfect for each other. I'm asking you to have a little faith and trust in me to preserve the customs and traditions you taught me. I've done everything you've asked of me literally all my life. I'm asking you not to disown me because I didn't go with your choice for the woman I want to be with for the rest of my life."

"You're making a mistake," Huan insisted.

"I'm in love with her!" He exploded. "And it's not a mistake just because you want it to be!"

"You want my blessing? You won't get it."

Huan turned his back to Tony.

"So that's it? You're really going to disown me?"

Tony stared at his father's back, waiting, hoping he would relent. But the silence dragged on, and each second that passed was like another punch in the gut. When the shock took over, numbing the pain, he stormed out the restaurant and to his car.

Inside, he stared at the restaurant door. This bridge was burning. He only hoped he could prevent the flames from reaching London.

∞∞∞∞∞∞∞

It was just shy of two pm when London stepped into New Sun Restaurant. Only three tables were occupied, but several others were still waiting to be bussed. Mrs. Yu was speaking with customers at one table, a stack of bill folders tucked under her arm.

Pleased with her timing, London headed toward a

table near the kitchen. She set the pie box down before taking a seat. Her phone vibrated as she sat, and she knew before she looked that it would be a message from Gianna or Valerie.

Smiling, she pulled out her phone to read the messages. They had been texting and planning to get together since Tony had dropped her off at her place that morning. She wanted to tell them how she felt about Tony in person.

Of course, she would rather tell Tony, but she wasn't sure he was ready for that just yet. His bold insistence that she was his could be an indication that he was, but words held power, and she wanted to give it a little more time before she shared hers.

Since she wasn't sure if Tony had told his mom about them dating yet, she shot Tony a text to let her know she was in the restaurant.

"London. What a surprise. How are you?"

London put her phone down and looked up at Mrs. Yu with a bright smile.

"I'm well. Fantastic, actually," she added with a grin. "How are you?"

"I'm well. Are you…Are you here alone?" Mrs. Yu asked, glancing at the door. "I see you brought Mr. Cheng a pie."

Her smile faltered a bit. Maybe Tony hadn't told her about their relationship yet. She bit her lip, realizing she should have thought this through before rushing over here. She made her plan to come here on a rollercoaster of emotion while logic waited, forgotten, on the ground.

She hadn't considered that Mrs. Yu didn't know or that showing up here expecting Tony to come have lunch with her would put him in an awkward position of introducing the woman he was dating to his mother long before he was ready to.

Reconsidering, she placed her hand on her phone and tried to brighten her smile.

"Uh, no. I just came to drop off the pie. It's been a while since I've been in to see you guys so I just thought that I would stop by."

"Oh. Well. Thank you," Mrs. Yu said, her voice just a tad bit nervous. "I'll take this back to Mr. Cheng. Thank you for coming by."

London blinked in surprised. Before she could find any words, Mrs. Yu had the pie in her hands and was walking to the kitchen.

"That was weird," she said quietly, ignoring the little ball of concern that knotted in her stomach.

But it *was* weird. And concerning. Mrs. Yu hadn't taken the pie back to Mr. Cheng in a long time. She always made him come out and get it. Mr. Cheng complied, feigning reluctance, but greeted her warmly when he saw her. What had changed?

Her phone vibrated beneath her hand. Lifting it, she saw that it was Tony calling her. Her stomach sank, and she realized that she had made a mistake after all. If he wasn't coming out, it meant that he wasn't ready to tell his parents about their relationship.

Feeling foolish, she stood. Before she could walk away, Mr. Cheng came barreling out of the kitchen, Mrs. Yu on his heels.

"Huan, don't do this!" Mrs. Yu shouted.

"I won't be bribed! He knew the consequences, and he made his choice. He has no business sending her here to try to bribe me."

His face red with anger, Huan dropped the pie on the table next to her. She looked up at him, met his eyes, and knew. Even before he said the words, she knew. His eyes were too angry for it to be anything else. Her heart, so full of love, burst and bled.

"You take this pie back to Tony and you tell him that this won't change my mind. So long as you two are together, he's not my son, and you're no longer welcome here."

Even knowing what was coming, the words struck her like a physical blow, and she took a full step backward in response.

Huan saw the shock and pain wash over her face and hardened his heart against any feeling except for anger and betrayal.

"Huan! How dare—"

"It's okay, Mrs. Yu," she interrupted, her voice thick with emotion.

They both froze and stared at her. Tamping down the tears, she fixed her gaze just over Mr. Cheng's shoulder before clearing her throat.

"Tony and I are no longer together. So. You don't have to worry. About anything."

London turned and walked out the door. She brought her phone up and saw that she had three missed calls from Tony. Ignoring them, she opened a ride share app to call for a ride and walked a full block away before she submitted her location.

She didn't want to be anywhere near the restaurant just in case she couldn't keep it together long enough to get home.

She was an idiot. Instead of trusting her instincts and steering clear of Tony, she fell for him. For those unique and creative gestures that made her change her mind about him. For the way he made her feel.

And it was all a lie.

She let the fury fill her. Let the feeling of betrayal surround her like a new skin. When her ride arrived, she summoned more anger until it sat on her so thickly that she didn't feel anything else.

When Tony called again, she considered going somewhere, anywhere that wasn't home. Her refusal to answer would lead him to assume that something had happened. He might have even talked to his parents. She knew that he would come after her and show up at her apartment.

But she refused to add insult to injury by avoiding her own home. When her ride arrived at her apartment, he was already there, as expected.

She thought that she was prepared for the flood of emotions that swamped her. Love. Attraction. Anger. Betrayal. Sorrow. Heartbreak.

Each slammed into the other in a vicious and brutal pile up that left her feeling shattered. He must know that she was bleeding and broken, but here he was, prepared to trample on the same broken pieces that he had come here to mend.

"I can explain," he began, barely waiting for her to get out of the car.

"Could have explained, you mean," she corrected, closing the car door. "Could have, but chose not to."

Her voice was devastatingly calm. She had to be furious. She had to be hurt. But she wasn't showing it, and the absence of emotion terrified him.

She just stood there, staring at him blankly. Was she already dismissing him?

"I know, I know, and I'm so sorry," he said. "But it's just my dad. My mom wants us to be together, remember? We just needed some time to get him to come around."

London narrowed her eyes. "Come around to what?"

He looked down at his feet, and she knew that he didn't want to answer that question. More, she could see his panic, the fear. How long had it been there? How long had he been lying to her to keep this exact moment from happening?

Elliot was right after all, and knowing it made her sick to her stomach.

"Be honest with me. Can you at least do that?"

"Yes, of course," he promised.

"Why didn't you ask me out that first night?"

Of course it would come to this. That first omission of truth. The lie that he had built the entire relationship on. Once exposed, everything would come crashing down, and his heart would burn right along with it.

"Because I thought my parents would disown me," he stepped forward when he saw tears well up in her eyes. "That's on me, London, and on my father. Not you. This is my choice, and his. You're everything I've always wanted. I knew it the day we met, and I couldn't let you go even knowing what it would cost me. That's my choice, and I don't regret it. I won't regret it."

She shook her head when a single tear slid down her cheek, and pursed her lips together before she let out a breath. He knew the truth would hurt her, but he wasn't prepared for how deeply it cut him to see her in pain. Pain that he had caused.

"I know I should have told you everything before but I…I just…I was afraid I'd lose you."

"So instead of being honest with me, you made me fa—" She cut herself off. He didn't get to know how she felt and she would see to it that she didn't feel that way much longer. "You need to leave."

She turned and headed to her apartment. He followed, worried that she would turn him away forever if he didn't take this chance to make things right.

"London, please."

"I can't believe that Elliot was right about you. You're exactly like him."

He winced when her words cut him. "I'm not like him."

She stopped and rounded on him, her eyes filled with anger now. "Aren't you? You both expect me to be okay with destroying your relationship with your parents just so we can be together!"

"You didn't destroy anything. Can we go inside and talk, please?"

"No. Leave. Now."

"London," he started, reaching toward her.

She slapped his hand away. "Don't touch me." Her breath hitched as she fought back tears. "Don't call me. Don't text me. Don't come here. Don't email me or show up at my job or send me tickets or flowers. Don't anything. From this day forward, as far as you're concerned, I don't even exist."

She went inside and slammed the door behind her, startling him. When he heard the lock click into place, he stumbled away. Every breath hurt. Every beat of his heart felt like a stab in the chest.

And because the pain was excruciating and the misery too intense, he sat in his car for the second time that day as everything he loved burned away.

CHAPTER 13

After she had closed the door, quite literally, on her relationship with Tony, she succumbed to the first wave of tears.

Dropping on the couch, she let the pain come as she sobbed. Memories washed over her, tainted now with the truth. She did her best to block them out, but they just kept coming.

This was worse, so much worse, than it had been with Elliot. She hadn't loved him. He had hurt her pride and wounded her spirit, but her heart had remained untouched. This time, there was no part of her that was unscathed.

When she was empty, she stared blankly at the ceiling, willing her head to stop throbbing enough to let her move. Her throat was painfully dry and her body felt like lead, but she wanted to be done. Needed to be done. She slowly eased off the couch and made her way to the bathroom.

Staring at her image, she surveyed the damage and deemed it absolutely pathetic.

Feeling the urge to cry again, she distracted herself by removing her make up with the designated moist toilette. Then she washed her face with cold water before taking another look at herself. She may look a little better, but she certainly didn't feel like it.

Moving into the kitchen, she pulled a facemask that she usually reserved for facials from the freezer. She sat for ten minutes with the mask over her eyes before she sent word to her friends that she and Tony were done.

Within hours Valerie, Gianna, and Iris had arrived at her home. She admitted that she was hurt and felt betrayed, but she couldn't bring herself to tell them that she had been foolish enough to fall in love with him. She wanted to keep that shame to herself.

So they cursed him, damned him, and had to convince Gianna not to slash his tires. When they finally left, she felt a little better. But when she lay in her bed, she swore she could smell him there. The scent brought back images of the times they had made love in that bed. And those images broke her.

London knew that she would have to use the rest of the weekend to wallow, to cry, to feel, and, most importantly, to heal.

She forced herself to wake up early the next morning and joined Valerie for Yoga in the Park at North Natomas Regional Park. The free Saturday event was hosted and organized by the district's council member each week and was a short ten-minute walk from Valerie's house.

It felt good, despite the July heat, to be under the sun, breathing fresh air while the scent of fresh cut grass surrounded her. Feeling centered, they wandered over to the farmers market just next door and she took care of her shopping for that week.

On Sunday, she treated herself to a full day at Asha Urban Baths. The old-world style wellness bathhouse boasted a sauna, steam room, and cold plunge. Unplugged from the outside world, everyone inside spoke in hushed tones while they lounged and relaxed.

There was peace and calm and quiet. Here her mind and body could unwind and rejuvenate. It was exactly what she needed.

Day by day, piece-by-piece, she made herself whole again. Her work kept her busy, her friends kept her entertained, and she found ways to stay distracted.

Her favorite distraction, and another favorite thing about living in Sacramento, was the California State Fair. It was the quintessential summer event in Sacramento, and drew crowds from all over the state. She lived for the food, the rides, the concerts, the shows, and even the hot summer nights.

Though they needed no reason to go to the state fair, they decided that it was the perfect place to celebrate Gianna passing her six-month probation at Intel. It didn't matter that she still had one week left. There was an unspoken agreement that they all needed something to celebrate.

So, dressed in short shorts and tank tops, Gianna, Valerie, and London wandered around the park drinking wine slushies and snacking on deep fried goodies. They stopped by the main concert stage and danced to Tony! Toni! Toné as they belted out their top hits. They wandered quietly through the photography exhibition before settling down with beer to watch the hypnotist make fools of her volunteers.

Under the bright and flashing lights of rides, they ate again and drank even more before settling down to watch the fireworks close out the fair for the night.

Enjoying the normalcy of the night, London found herself feeling better than she had in weeks. Life went on, and as long as she learned from this lesson, things were bound to get better from here.

"Thanks for driving, Val," London said as they walked to her car.

"Thanks for paying for parking. I can't believe it's up to $15 now."

"Worth it!" Gianna interjected. "You know how I feel about bacon wrapped anything."

Valerie laughed. "The girl loves her pork."

"Oink, oink," Gianna snorted. "Would have been better if Tony! Toni! Toné! wasn't playing tonight. Much as I love their songs, I now have the urge to kick in a certain Tony's balls."

London rolled her eyes. "Didn't even make that connection until just now."

"Me either," Valerie shared, unlocking her car and climbing in. "But now that we're talking about Tony."

"No thanks," London said from the backseat.

Gianna turned in her seat as Valerie backed out of their spot. She glared at London.

"We've given you two weeks to come clean, so really, this conversation is long overdue."

London tilted her head in confusion. "Come clean about what?"

"The fact that you're in love with Tony," Valerie said quietly.

She blinked. "What makes you think that?"

"You had us practically foaming at the mouth for whatever thing that you could only tell us in person," Gianna began. "And then when we get there, you tell us that it's over. I don't know about you, Val, but I know what I expected to hear, and that wasn't it."

"I was expecting happy news," Valerie admitted.

"It could have been…" London trailed off, not knowing what else to say. She stared out the window instead, realizing that there was no point in denying it.

"I'll get over it."

"Does he know?" Valerie asked.

"No." She didn't want to talk about this. "Why does it matter? It's over."

"Well if you're both pining over each other, it can't actually be over," Gianna said.

"Well it is, so—" She stopped. "How do you know that he's pining over me?"

Gianna gave an annoyed sigh. "Watching you pretend not to be miserable has just really riled me up, and you know I promised to kick his ass if he hurt you so I may have gone to his house last Saturday to do just that."

"Oh. My. Gawd." London said, holding her head in her hands. "How did you even get his address?"

"She did the invites for my wedding," Valerie recalled. "I just knew that decision would come back to bite somebody in the ass."

"At least it wasn't yours!"

"Somehow that doesn't comfort me."

"Anyway. He completely ruined it for me," Gianna complained. "Came to the door looking like Luke Skywalker after Vader kicked his ass. Looked like he lost weight too, and not in a flattering way. Before I could cuss him out, he asked 'How is she?' I've never seen anything so pathetic in my life."

"Good. Great," London said flatly. "I'm glad he's miserable."

"Hey, me too, but I was hoping to at least be part of the reason."

Valerie slanted Gianna a hard look. "I think what Gianna means to say is, maybe you should talk to him?"

"Yes. That," Gianna agreed, pointing to Valerie.

"Give him a false sense of hope so I can tear him down."

"Gianna!"

She looked over at Valerie, her face all innocence. "What?"

Valerie rolled her eyes. "Look, London. I'm not suggesting that you forgive him for not being truthful, at least before he's tried to earn back your trust. But maybe, since you both obviously have strong feelings for each other, you should consider giving him another chance."

"How can you say that?" London demanded. "How can I be with him knowing it would ruin his relationship with his father? Would you have stayed with Jun if his parents hadn't approved of you two being together?"

"Jun has family who don't approve, and some outright shunned his parents as a result. It's been hard on them, Jun included, but they're dealing with it."

"I'm so sorry, Val," London said, her heart breaking a little. "I didn't know."

Valerie shrugged as if it wasn't a big deal. "I catch people, black people and Asian people, staring at us in confusion, in disgust. There is always going to be someone who doesn't approve. We face it, and all of the consequences, together."

"But we're talking about his dad."

"He wouldn't be the first person in the history of this country whose family turned their back on their own child for choosing to be with someone who wasn't of the same ethnicity," Valerie said softly.

Gianna snorted. "I say screw anybody who doesn't approve, parents included. Tony and I seem to see eye to eye on that, and I give him kudos there. It's the only thing I like about him right now."

"It couldn't have been easy for him to have that conversation with his dad when he knew that there was a chance that he wouldn't approve."

"Val, please stop trying to make me feel sorry for the guy," Gianna complained.

London sat quietly while they argued, thinking it through. She had thought of all those things that they had both said. She knew all of it. But for some reason, she still couldn't bring herself to look past any of it to be with Tony. There was some block, some emotion, something that kept her firmly if not foolishly rooted on this path.

"I know it's not what you want, London, but life isn't always fair," Valerie said with a small sigh. "Sometimes we get lucky and get close to having it all, and sometimes we're so far from that we might as well be on another planet. You have a chance to find some middle ground between those two, and we just want to make sure you don't pass that up."

"Just think about," Gianna suggested.

London sat silently for the remainder of the ride, thinking about little else.

∞∞∞∞∞∞∞∞∞

Tony awoke on his stomach, the side of his face plastered against the sheets. Sunlight assaulted his eyes and burned his retinas. Squeezing them shut again, he willed away the painful throbbing at his temples.

Sunlight wake up call meant it was the weekend. He hated weekends.

It was easier, much easier, to find things to occupy his time during the week. Even though August wasn't a particularly busy month for events and concerts at the Golden 1 Center, there was always work to be done.

There was always a need for sponsors, and he dove in to finding, attracting, and solidifying those relationships. Sometimes it meant catching a quick flight to Los Angeles or driving all over Sacramento, but he didn't mind. It kept him occupied. It kept him focused.

He spent more time with the sales and marketing teams than he ever had in the past, brainstorming new ideas, images, and proposals. He even delved into the archives in order to review past strategies. They wanted to be innovative and fresh, and he felt it was important to make sure they weren't just repackaging previous marketing techniques.

When they did have events, he bounced from suite to suite, chatting with guests and just trying to make sure everyone was satisfied. Repeat clients really enjoyed the glad handling, and for once, he was happy to oblige.

It often meant that he worked twelve-hour days, and after hours and hours of putting coffee and energy drinks into his system, he was rarely tired at the end of it.

His solution? The gym.

Most nights he could join somebody for a game or two of basketball. If he wasn't up for that, he just lifted or jogged until his body signaled that it had had enough. If he had enough energy, he showered before going to bed, but most of the time he just collapsed on the bed and succumbed to exhaustion.

Which was exactly what he had done last night.

Unfortunately, it wasn't always easy to find

something palatable to do on the weekends. He quickly discovered that he hated being out in public. There were far too many couples holding hands or embracing or kissing. He hadn't handled seeing those easy displays of affection after the incident, so he just gave up on going anywhere that promised to have more than ten people.

He usually slept half of the day away, the sixty-hour workweek finally catching up to him and keeping him down for the count. If he had remembered to close the damn curtains when he came home last night, he would still be sleep.

Tony opened his eyes again to scowl at the window and saw his shorts on the floor where he had dropped them after closing the curtains.

He had closed them! So why were they—

"Rise and shine, sleeping beauty," Jun said sweetly, interrupting Tony's thoughts.

Freezing cold water shocked his system, sending him flying off the bed in protest. He fell flat on his ass on the side of the bed and bumped his head against the closet door. Dripping wet, his body throbbing and shivering, he glared up at Jun, who was holding his sides as he laughed uncontrollably.

"What the fuck is wrong with you?" He demanded, staring at his soaked bed. His largest pot sat there surrounded by ice cubes. "Did you fucking put ice in the water?"

Jun started to speak, but kept laughing instead. Tony scowled and pushed himself off the floor. Once on his feet, he peeled off his soaked shirt and tossed it on the bed.

Jun wiped tears from his eyes as the laughter began to subside.

"You didn't wake after I opened the curtains, so I figured you needed some extra encouragement. I dumped your entire tray of ice in the pot by the way. My only regret is not recording. What the hell was I thinking? Ah, well. I'll just have to remember this moment forever."

"Great. Now that you've had your fun, can you let yourself out?"

Jun rocked on his heels. "Nope."

Tony glared at him. "I need to get dressed."

"Think of this as the boys locker room. Don't worry, I won't look."

"What the hell are you doing here anyway?"

Jun looked down the hallway while Tony rummaged through a pile of clothes on his dresser for what he assumed would be a cleanish pair of shorts and a shirt.

"You won't answer my text or calls."

"I've been busy at work," Tony pointed out, pulling on his shorts. "I don't think that warrants an ice bath."

"You know, I would have believed that sack of bullshit, if not for your little confession about avoiding me when I started dating Valerie. So I know that what's really going on is that you're avoiding me because London dumped your stupid ass and it's too hard for you to see me with my wife."

Her name brought a torrent of pain. The memories that he kept at bay with work and caffeine and exercise and *anything* but thinking about her came flooding back. The first time he saw her. The first time he heard her sexy voice. The first time that she smiled at him. The first time he heard her laugh.

He remembered everything in between until he was viciously fast forwarded through every moment that would end up being the last. And now that he was thinking the thoughts that he had tried so damn hard not to think and reliving memories that now made it difficult to breathe, he became keenly aware of every part of his mind, body, and heart that hurt.

He closed his eyes and tried to will away the pain.

"You need to leave."

"I've given you a month to get your head out of your ass, and I'm done waiting. I want my friend back."

"So back off. Give me time." Tony stormed from the room, and then stopped when he saw the pizza box on the kitchen island. "You brought food?"

"And the beer is in the fridge," Jun said, clapping Tony on the back. "Let's sit and get this shit out in the open. You'll feel better after."

Annoyed and reeling from the pain, Tony sighed and sat. Stubborn Jun was a rare sight, and he didn't have the energy to deal with it and get him gone. The sooner he gave Jun what he wanted, the sooner he would go away.

So he told him what went down between mouthfuls of food. Once he was done, he had to admit that he did feel a little better. He had been avoiding everyone since it happened. Jun, Oliver, his parents. He hadn't been able to bring himself to talk to anyone that mattered. Just closed himself in to close off the hurt.

"Rough hand you've been dealt, man," Jun sympathized. "And then you fucked it up royally."

"Understatement," Tony replied. "I should have been up front with her from the beginning."

"So be up front with her now."

Tony drank more beer. "She made it very clear that any future advances on my part are unwanted. And hell, after everything that happened, respecting this last request is the least I could do. She deserves it."

"So you're just going to let her go?"

"What other choice do I have? She barely trusted me when we first started getting together. She's got no reason to trust me now."

Jun shrugged. "I don't know, dude, but if you love her, you have to find a way to make it work. You and your dad aren't going to have the same relationship going forward, if you have one at all. You have nothing left to lose."

"I wouldn't even know where to start," Tony confessed.

"You know, it's a bit of a wild idea, but maybe you should be honest with her," Jun said dryly.

"Obviously. But before I can do that, she has to be willing to see me."

"Hey, I can't come up with all the answers for you," Tony said, rising from his chair to clean up. "You'll figure it out."

"Have you seen her? Is she..." he trailed off, looking around as if he could pull the word out of thin air. "I don't know. I want her to be okay, but then that would mean that she was completely over me and that's the last thing I want."

"Yeah, I get that. I haven't seen her. Val says she's okay, but she said it in a way that makes me think that Val doesn't believe her."

"Shit. If she's still hurting, then she's not going to want to see me."

Jun lifted his eyebrows. "If she's still hurting, then she's not over you."

"Yeah, that's true too," he said thoughtfully, hope blooming in his chest.

"I'd love to stay and finish those beers, but this place smells like you haven't cleaned it in a month."

"Because I haven't," Tony grinned, only slightly embarrassed. Then he sighed. "It's been a rough month."

"Guess you gotta get your shit together before you go get your girl. I'll leave you to it," he said, turning toward the door. He stopped suddenly and turned back. "Oh, but if you try to cut me out again, I will hurt you. That's not how this shit works."

Now he felt like shit. "I'm sorry for that, Jun. I appreciate you coming over here to knock some sense into me."

"I'll forgive you since London dumped your sorry ass. Next pizza and beer is on you," he called out as he left.

Tony looked around his apartment and barely recognized the space. His kitchen counters were littered with an assortment of take out bags, containers, and wrappers. It was a miracle that the place hadn't been infested with ants.

The living room was in an equally sad state. Much to his embarrassment, he had started stacking disposable cups together on his coffee table. He assumed that the bag next to the cups was filled with lids and straws.

PlayStation remotes, discs, and cases sat haphazardly on the television console along with his headsets. He hoped none of his games had gotten scratched up in his carelessness.

He wasn't a neat freak, but he wasn't a slob either. It was pretty pathetic that he was quickly approaching slob territory. Sighing, he rose and decided to tackle the kitchen first.

As he filled a trash bag, he tried to figure out what to do about London. He had to tell her that he loved her, but knew that it wouldn't matter if she wasn't able or willing to accept that he wouldn't have a relationship with his father if he chose her.

He respected and loved that she didn't want to come between them, but this chasm had been growing between them long before she came along. How could he get her to understand that?

How could he get her to understand that while he might be losing his father, he would be gaining so, so much more by being with the woman he loved?

He turned on the water before he went to his door to drop the trash bag there and wondered if she would listen if he begged.

He wasn't above begging. He plugged the sink and added soap. Finding a fresh towel, he started wiping down the counters as he considered doing just that.

He was desperate enough to give it a try, but he had to find some way to get her to agree to give him the time of day. Despite having more information about her than he had when he first started pursuing her, he found himself at a complete loss.

She could toss, delete, or decline anything he sent her. He couldn't accidently bump into her anywhere near her job, and even if he could, he would embarrass them both trying to talk to her in front of complete strangers.

Moving into his bedroom to strip his bed, he decided that he needed to orchestrate a private meeting. But since there was no way he could do that on his own, that would have to be the last phase of this plan at least.

He needed help, and that meant he would have to patch up a few other relationships first. He knew that Jun was on his side, but he wasn't sure how Valerie felt.

She couldn't be happy that he hurt her friend. He already knew how Gianna felt. If she hadn't pitied him when she showed up a few weeks ago then she would have already kicked his ass.

The ass kicking might be worth it if he got London back.

Considering it, and the new idea that was beginning to take shape, Tony continued to clean and let his mind work.

CHAPTER 14

London glanced up from where she sat on the couch when she heard the soft, tentative knock at her door. Sitting up, she paused her movie. She wasn't expecting any packages or company, so she wondered who it could be.

Probably someone at the wrong address, she thought, rising from the couch and walking to the door.

She looked through the peephole and then jumped back. Heart racing, she stared wide eyed at the door and tried to process the fact that Tony's mother stood on the other side of it.

It hurt. She had grown particularly fond of her relationship with Mrs. Yu, and it hurt to realize just how much she had missed her. It hurt knowing that that relationship was over.

Mrs. Yu knocked again, but she just stood their staring at the door. Should she open it or pretend that she wasn't home? Would she go away? Did she want her to go away? Why was she here?

She was a mess. An actual mess, she realized, looking down at herself. It was Saturday, and she was having a Star Wars marathon while wearing super short BB-8 shorts and a sports bra. Since her studio was on the older side, she only had an AC wall unit, and it barely did much during the hot August days.

There was a knock again, and it was more insistent. As if Mrs. Yu knew she was inside. Shit.

"Just a minute!"

London rushed into the bathroom. She splashed cold water on her face, hoping it would erase some of the shock. Dashing out, she dialed down the AC as low as it would go and put her room fan on high. Then she pulled open her closet and grabbed the first dress she saw.

She pulled it on as she approached the front door. Then she took a deep breath before she opened it.

Mrs. Yu wore a pretty dress the color of the sky. Her hair was pulled back and tied at her neck. It was the first time she saw her outside of her restaurant attire. Not that she wore a uniform, but she never saw her so casually dressed before.

"I'm sorry for the unexpected visit," Mrs. Yu smiled cautiously. "I came to talk to you. If…if that's okay."

A heavy weight settled on her heart as she wondered why she was here. There was a strange, determined look in Mrs. Yu's eyes, as if she was a woman on a mission.

London narrowed her eyes and spoke quietly in Mandarin. "Did Tony send you?"

"Not exactly. I insisted that he give me your address so I could send you some food," she admitted, holding the bag up. "I didn't tell him that I was planning to bring it myself. I don't think he would have approved."

"Is this about Tony?"

"Not exactly," Mei said with a smile. "May I come in?"

She wanted to say no. She wanted to say yes. She

ended up saying nothing and stepping to the side so she could enter.

Mei took in the U shaped studio apartment as she entered. A small, quaint kitchen was on her left and a bar height table for two sat in the space on her right. The walls were lined with bookshelves, and those were filled to the brim with figurines and other toys that she didn't recognize.

She had squeezed in a television stand between the shelves, and Mei saw that she had interrupted whatever London had been watching. As they approached the couch, Mei saw that there was a full sized bed tucked up against the far wall.

"Uhm…can I get you anything? Some water?" London asked.

"That would be nice. These egg rolls should go in the fridge," Mei advised, handing her the bag. "You can fry them up when you're ready."

"Thank you," she said, taking the bag and going to her kitchen.

Mei sat on the couch. "I came here to try to get your forgiveness."

Baffled, London gaped at her when she came to join her on the couch. "Forgive you? For what? You didn't do anything."

"Huan is a difficult and stubborn man," she said, accepting the glass of water. "But that does not excuse how he spoke to you, or how he treated you. I'm sorry for it. I have not forgiven him for it yet and I don't expect you to either. I'm sorry for putting you in such an uncomfortable situation."

"Mrs. Yu—"

"Tony told me about your ex, how horribly he treated you, and about his parent's expectations," Mei continued. "Huan has different reasons for not approving of the two of you being together. But I knew that, and I had every intention of setting you two up despite that. I only thought of what I felt was good for Tony. I never considered how being put in the middle of such family drama would impact you."

Mei paused to sip water and shake her head.

"I was so sure that Huan would come around that I didn't realize that he could hurt you. Had I thought of it…"

She trailed off and took a moment to meet London's shocked eyes.

"I would like to say that I would have given up on you and Tony being together, but that would be a lie. Even now, it's still what I want. I'm sorry that I let my wants hurt you."

"Mrs. Yu, you've done nothing wrong," London assured her. "What happened between Tony and I…it's unfortunate, but that's not on you."

"What's the difference between Tony and I? We both wanted the same outcome. For you two to be together, no matter the consequences."

"But why?" London demanded, her eyes beginning to water in her confusion. "Why would you want us to be together when it would rip your family apart? Why would I be okay with doing that? I…I can't do that. You guys…you guys mean too much to me."

Mei set her glass on the coffee table took London's hand. "You haven't ripped this family apart. When Huan and I came here, we weren't always treated with kindness. Huan grew a thick skin, and drew a hard line against anyone who didn't look like him in self-defense. When we had Tony, he softened, but he has been slow to let go of the armor that helped him get through some difficult times.

"You haven't ripped this family apart." She said it with feeling this time, trying to drive her point home. "You and Tony forced Huan to drop his last bit of armor. He lashed out at you, and at Tony, because the sudden change was so uncomfortable. It doesn't excuse his behavior. We all have every right to be upset with him. But once it passes, we can all heal together if we can all forgive each other. I hope that you'll forgive me. And Tony. And Huan. Eventually."

"I don't know what to say," she confessed, pulling her hand away to stand up. Then she sat again, not sure what to do with herself. "I didn't think of it that way. But I've never blamed you for any of this. It's easy for me to forgive you and Mr. Cheng, but Tony…I just can't get there for some reason."

"I understand," Mei said, rising. "You need time, just as Huan does, to listen to what is in your heart. To accept it, or to let go. Take what you need, and know that we'll be waiting for you when you're ready."

∞∞∞∞∞∞∞

"So do you think that she'll forgive me?"

Tony stared at the window while he listened to his mother on the phone. It had been two days since she executed phase one of his plan. He supposed phase one was really her plan. Since she cared for London as deeply as he did, his mother had been eager to patch up their relationship.

Not that he minded. He was willing to do anything to get her back.

"Only time will tell," she told him.

Unfortunately, he was afraid that if he gave her

more time then she would get over him, and he was entirely too selfish to let her do that.

Tony paced his hallway while Jun lounged on his couch, sipping on a beer.

"I have to hope that speaking to my mom helped."

Jun shrugged. "They did have a relationship long before you came along and wrecked it all."

Tony scowled at him. "Thank you for reminding me."

"My pleasure."

Tony thought about flipping him off, but since he needed his help for phase two of his plan, he resisted the urge. He sat on the couch next to Jun and picked up his own beer.

"I need you and Valerie to throw a Labor Day party. Get us all together again."

"You plan on hashing things out with her at my house?" Jun asked, his face conveying his doubt in the possibility of that working out.

"No, of course not. I'm banking on this party opening the door to get her to talk to me."

"Explain," Jun demanded.

Tony set his beer down and rose to pace again.

"We're best friends, so of course you'll invite me. But you'll feel worried about me and London being around each other after the thing that happened," Tony explained.

"I will?"

"Yes. My fuck up puts you and Val between a rock and a hard place. You invite me, but not London or vice versa. So you'll bring it up to her, get her thoughts on it."

Jun glared at him. "Shit. This really does fuck things up for us. You bastard."

"Absolutely," Tony agreed, continuing to pace. "So you wonder if London and I can work out some sort of truce. You promise to talk to me about checking the drama at the door and maybe even encourage me to clear the air with London. Maybe Val can have a similar conversation with London."

"You're hoping Val will get London to agree to see you so you can beg her to take your sorry ass back. It's sneaky," Jun said. "I'm in."

Tony stopped pacing to look at him. "Do you think Val will get on board?"

Jun shrugged. "Probably. She's not your biggest fan right now, but she also isn't rooting for you to lose."

"That's more than I deserve, so you won't hear me complaining." He plopped down on the couch. "I really need this to work. If she agrees to see me, then I have to believe that a part of her still cares about me. If she didn't, she wouldn't need to talk to me. There would be nothing to clear up. She would have no problem being around me. She did it with her ex for years and only Iris knew about it."

"I still can't believe it. The girl must have nerves of steel."

"And that's why I have to go all out in the final phase of my plan. I have to beg, plead, grovel, romance her, and convince her to at least consider trusting me enough to let me earn her forgiveness."

Jun clucked his tongue. "Sounds impossible."

"Living without her is impossible. This is just the hard part."

Jun grinned. "Alright. Tell me about this plan."

∞∞∞∞∞∞∞

Today was the day.

Tony walked nervous laps around the upstairs breezeway of Downtown Commons as he waited for London to arrive. He'd chosen what he hoped seemed like a very neutral and public location for this meeting but used his connections to make it private.

It cost him more money than the Kings tickets had, but he had no regrets. The stage was set, and every little detail was checked and rechecked. He had about thirty minutes before she arrived and he was certain that he would use that time to panic and stress and overthink everything.

He was going to be a mess when she got here.

But she was coming, and that meant something. Valerie and Jun's Labor Day party was three days away, and this was the only chance he was going to get to smooth things over with London.

He hoped he could.

Taking a deep breath, he turned to go inside the shop and saw his father standing by the door, watching him.

Tony hadn't seen him since that morning, and refused his mother's pleas to talk to or meet him. He was so sure that he would still be angry with him, but seeing him now, all he felt was pity.

Their relationship would be over, and he pitied the loss that would bring them both.

"Uhm…what are you doing here?" Tony asked as he approached him.

Huan shifted on his feet. "I came to see London."

He blinked. "Uh…what?"

"Your ma said she would meet you here today and I wanted to make sure you knew…and that she knew…"

Tony stepped closer and searched his dad's face. "Knew what?"

"That it's fine. You and her being together. It's fine. And me and you…we're okay," Huan huffed out an annoyed breath. "You're lucky to have her. Go inside. She'll be here soon and I want to talk to her first."

Relief flooded through him, and he felt like he could do anything. "Bà, we're both lucky."

∞∞∞∞∞∞∞

She had amazing friends.

They listened without judgment, shared deep and personal thoughts without shame, supported her through every minor and major bump in life, brought her so much joy and happiness, and were the biggest pains in the ass.

London didn't want to see Tony, but because of her friends, she was on her way to Downtown Commons to do just that. Thanks to their well-meaning intentions, she caved and agreed to meet up with him to clear the air.

They knew that she wasn't ready, and that only made them push her harder. She needed this closure, they insisted, in order to truly begin to move on and move forward.

But what they didn't realize was that she was deathly afraid that if she saw him again, she never would.

She understood where Jun and Valerie were coming from. Their break up had put them in the difficult position of having to choose sides. They didn't deserve that, and she wanted to make it right.

She just needed a few more months.

Unfortunately, she wasn't going to get it. When the

ride share pulled up to DOCO to drop her off, she accepted her fate and climbed out with a heavy sigh.

She had agreed to meet Tony after she got off work and had been grateful when he had suggested a public space. Public hopefully meant that they would both be civil enough to avoid making complete fools of themselves.

She crossed the plaza where people mingled, took pictures in front of the Golden 1 Center, or lounged in chairs. RareTea was located on the second floor of the outdoor shopping center. She had heard of the popular boba spot, but hadn't had a chance to try it yet. As she rode the escalator, she wondered what she would get. Then she glanced up and froze.

Mr. Cheng stood at the top of the escalator, blotting sweat from his face with a small towel. When he saw her, he snapped to attention and shoved the towel in his pocket. He adjusted his grip nervously on the white bag he held in both of his hands while he waited for her.

London stepped off to the side when she reached the top. More than a little surprised to see him here, she didn't speak. Questions raced through her head instead. What was he doing here? Did Tony set this up? Who was running the restaurant? What did he want? What was he holding? What was going on?

He seemed equally unsure of what to say and stared at her for a moment before he seemed to remember what he was there for.

"Here," he said, holding out the bag. "Your usual order."

London blinked. "What?"

"This would be much faster if you didn't interrupt me," he complained, but his voice was soft and gentle.

Remembering how often he had used those exact words, her eyes began to tear up.

"Next time, come to the restaurant. I…I miss…the pie."

London gave a watery laugh then let out a shaky breath. "Are you sure?"

Huan again held out the bag. "Next time you stop by, bring Tony. I have to get back to the restaurant."

London took the bag and nearly broke when he gave her a small smile.

"Don't let me keep you. Thank you for the meal."

"Thank you," he said, and walked away.

Alone, London took a moment to compose herself. So much for not making a fool of herself, she thought dryly, wiping her face with her free hand. If she didn't get it together, this meeting wasn't going to go well.

She hadn't been expecting that. It wasn't an outright apology or his blessing, but she knew that's what he meant. He had his own way of communicating his feelings to her, just as he had since they first met.

Which meant the last roadblock was gone. Tony's parents were no longer one of the reasons that they couldn't be together.

Distracted by her thoughts, she didn't think anything of the blinds that covered RareTea's windows and doors. She opened the door and had one foot inside before she completely froze again.

White, black, gray, and blue balloons hung from every wall and from the counter. There were blue and white flower petals on the floor and a large bouquet in the same color on one of the small square tables. On another table, a R2-D2 figurine sat next to a blue light saber. The March of the Resistance played on the speakers.

Tony stood in the center of it all wearing a white shirt with Princess Leia's face above the words "I love you."

"Oh, fuck," she said, dropping her bag on the floor.

His hair was slightly longer, and even with the cautious and concerned expression that filled his face, he was impossibly more good looking than she had remembered. Her heart broke. Her heart yearned. She couldn't do this.

When she started to take a step back, he launched forward and pulled her back inside.

"Wait. Please, wait. Hear me out," he begged.

"This is…I…no. I can't."

Tony pulled the door closed and locked it. She looked up at him in disbelief.

"You agreed to talk to me," he reminded her.

"To talk yes. This," she gestured wildly around the room, her heart practically stabbing her chest. "This was not what I meant."

"Okay. What did you mean?" He asked patiently.

"Our friends are asking us to get along and to be courteous in each other's company for their sake. Obviously you can't do that."

"No, I can't. I can't pretend that what we had never happened. Pretend that it was nothing. I won't do that."

"Don't be so selfish," she demanded, moving away from him. "You need to open that door. Right now."

"I'm being selfish?" He asked, closing the distance between them. "You won't let me apologize. You won't let me explain. You just shut me out. Now you're telling me to ignore how I feel."

"You can feel however you want to feel," she insisted, skirting away from him to go back to the door.

"I'm only suggesting you ignore it when we're in the same room, for the sake of our friends."

"No. Fuck that."

"Look—"

Tony grabbed her. "Fuck that. I'm in love with you. Nothing else matters but you. Not Jun, not my parents. Just you."

She squeezed her eyes shut, refusing to look at him. "You can't walk away from your childhood friend—"

"I can," he interrupted.

"Or turn your back on your family—"

"I will."

"I won't talk to you when you're being unreasonable."

"Too fucking bad. You're being pretty unreasonable too." He pushed her down into a chair when she tried to push him away and leaned down in front of her. "I'm willing to lose everything except you. That's how much I love you. But I trust that my friends and family will respect that and what I hope we have together. You can keep shutting me out or pushing me away, but I won't ever stop fighting for you until I've rebuilt what we had."

"You're not being fair," she said angrily, refusing to look at him.

"No," he whispered. "I love you too much to be fair."

She closed her eyes. "Stop saying that."

"You might as well get used to it. I'm going to keep telling you I love you until you believe it."

She finally looked at him. "I believe it."

Tony touched her face gently, brushing the tears away with his thumb. "Then why are you crying?"

"I'm not crying," she lied.

He wanted to kiss her, but thought it might be too soon. "I know I hurt you. I know that you're afraid to trust me. To love me. I'm sorry. I was afraid to lose you and I made a mess of what we had. You're everything I've ever wanted."

"Please stop," she begged.

"I won't. I won't lie or hide the truth ever again. Let me earn your trust again. Let me earn your love. Give me four weeks."

"Tony, please."

"My mother loves you."

"You're so unfair."

"How about three weeks?" He asked, taking her face in his hands.

"Did you tell your dad to come here?"

He shook his head. "No. He surprised me too. I wasn't expecting it, but he said he wanted to talk to you. What did he say?" She gestured to the bag that sat on the floor by the door. "He brought my favorite dish."

"Really? I swear I had nothing to do with that. We talked, literally right before you showed up, but I didn't tell him that I was meeting you here. My mom did." Tony grinned. "So about those three weeks…"

"Two. That's it."

Tony struggled to keep his hands gentle as he checked the urge to jump up and down like an idiot.

"We'll revisit these terms at the end of the two weeks?"

"Tony," she warned.

"Okay, okay. I can rebuild a bridge in two weeks. But first, you're going to need this."

Tony stood and reached around the counter. He shook out the shirt and held it front of him, revealing the image of Han Solo with the words "I know" written beneath.

London shook her head, trying not to grin. "You got it backwards."

"I know," he said with a grin. "But I figured the situation demanded I switch. That is unless you have something to say…"

She sighed, looked around the room, and then back at the man that had put all this together to win her back.

"I love you," she whispered.

He smiled. "I know."

ABOUT THE AUTHOR

Born and (mostly) raised in Sacramento, California in the 1980s, the world was my oyster. I grew up in a wonderfully culturally diverse neighborhood and as a result, I had a friend from (and a crush on) every ethnic group. And then, thanks to the advent of personal computers and dial up Internet, my world grew even bigger. I spent a lot of time in front of my computer watching anime, chatting on AIM messenger or chat rooms, downloading music from Napster, and writing poetry and fan fiction.

Naturally, this shaped me and kept my mind open and accepting. And love? That was maybe the one thing that was actually colorblind.

But as life would show me over the next several decades, love is a little more nuanced than that. So with my ever-increasing interest in the written language, I wrote about it. And drawn back to Sacramento, one of America's most diverse cities, I felt the need to dedicate a space that celebrated not only love, but this wonderfully diverse place that no one outside of California seems to know is the capital.

I want you to get to know my city, and maybe, you'll fall in love with the 916 too.

DD DAVIS

#SACRAMENTO

SACRAMENTO, CA

visitsacramento.com

Sacramento is the star on the map of California - where you will find cultural attractions to inspire you, cutting-edge cuisine to impress you, history to enrich you and surprises to put a smile on your face. Venture out in any direction and you'll see why we're so fond of saying, "California begins here."

Driving from Sacramento to:
- Napa Valley Wine Country, ~1 hour
- San Francisco, ~1.5 hours
- Lake Tahoe Ski Resorts, ~2 hours
- Yosemite National Park, ~2.5 hours

Flying from Sacramento to:
- Los Angeles, ~1 hour
- Las Vegas, ~ 1.5 hours
- San Diego, ~1.5 hours
- Hawaii, ~5 hours

CHASING OLIVES PHOTOGRAPHY

chasingolivesphotography.com

We are Chasing Olives Photography, a husband and wife partnership. On-location portrait photography in natural light is our favorite -- but we do so much more! We believe everyone should have beautiful photos, so we provide stunning, high-quality pictures at a very affordable rate. We serve Sacramento and the surrounding areas. We photograph engagements, families, maternity, headshots, seniors, and even pets (just to name a few)! We also photograph small events!

TOWER BRIDGE
www.expedia.com/Tower-Bridge-Central-Sacramento.d6063269.Vacation-
Attraction?pwaLob=wizard-package-pwa
A Californian icon and a feat of engineering, this is Sacramento's most photographed bridge. Its golden frame is especially striking when lit up at night.

When the California sun casts its first light over Sacramento's streets, the golden glow of the Tower Bridge matches that of the cupola on the State Capitol nearby. As the day progresses, thousands of people use the bridge to cross between Downtown and West Sacramento. Drive or walk across one of the country's official historic treasures.

For a closer look, stroll across Tower Bridge for views over the Sacramento River and watch the boats go by.

Tower Bridge is seen by many locals as the gateway to California's historic past, as it guides people to the heart of Old Sacramento's Victorian-era cathedral and State Capitol. Note the golden sheen of the bridge's paint symbolizing the California Gold Rush that made this capital's successful development possible.

Head back to the riverbanks near the bridge at dusk, when the tower outlines become more pronounced and floodlights come on. The bridge suddenly looks like a golden beacon against the darkening skies. After a River Cats baseball game at Raley Field, you may even see fireworks behind the bridge at night.

Sacramento's Tower Bridge is a public crossing and can be visited any time, day and night.

ELLA DINING ROOM AND BAR
elladiningroomandbar.com
A Downtown Sacramento institution and premier dining destination, Ella Dining Room and Bar serves New American, farm-to-fork cuisine for lunch, dinner and happy hour, featuring entrees of seafood, steaks, and pastas, small plates, salads, fresh oysters and traditional caviar service. Ella also features an award-winning wine list as well as seasonal and classic hand crafted cocktails at its renowned bar.

DISABILITY RIGHTS CALIFORNIA
downtownsac.org
 Disability Rights California (DRC) is the agency designated under federal law to protect and advocate for the rights of Californians with disabilities.

We work in litigation, legal representation, advocacy services, investigations, public policy, and provide information, advice, referral, and community outreach.

For more than 40 years, DRC has worked to advance the rights of Californians with disabilities in education, employment, independence, health, and safety, and has grown into the largest disability rights organization in the nation.

GOLDEN 1 CENTER
golden1center.com
Golden 1 Center sits proudly in the heart of downtown Sacramento, less than a mile from California's first thriving business district.

It's here that you'll find people from all walks of life building a community around their favorite things: Music, sports, entertainment, culture, food, and beverage. A homage to the city's legacy and a marvel of its bright future, Golden 1 Center represents everything that makes Sacramento the next Great American City. From design to sustainability to connectivity to cuisine, it's a celebration of what Sacramento does best.

ARCO ARENA
Located north of Sacramento's downtown, Arco Arena was built in 1985. It was home to the NBA's Sacramento Kings until Golden 1 Center opened in 2016. Although the arena has had two name changes (currently Sleep Train Arena and formally Power Balance Pavilion), many Sacramentans still refer to it as Arco.

SACRAMENTO KINGS
www.nba.com/kings
The Sacramento Kings are an American professional basketball team.

SACRAMENTO MONARCHS

www.sportsteamhistory.com/sacramento-monarchs

The Sacramento Monarchs were a basketball team based in Sacramento, California. They played in the Women's National Basketball Association (WNBA) from 1997 until folding on November 20, 2009. They played their home games at ARCO Arena.

CAFETERIA 15L

www.cafeteria15l.com

Cafeteria 15L is Sacramento's favorite comfort and eclectic urban restaurant offering American comfort cuisine with a classic flair. Designed by the designers of W Hotels, Cafeteria 15L features two plush outdoor patios, comfortable lounge space and large areas dedicated to private and semi-private dining in addition to the main dining room. Traditional dishes are created with a twist to evoke the nostalgia and comfort of a home-cooked meal.

MIDTOWN FARMERS MARKET

exploremidtown.org/midtown-farmers-market

This free, family-friendly market takes place year-round, every Saturday, on 20th street between J and L streets. The Midtown Farmers Market showcases local agriculture, prepared foods, and artisans and crafters while providing an opportunity for Midtown residents and business owners to discover regionally grown foods. Anchored in the heart of Midtown, the market serves as a lively and fun gathering place where Sacramentans can come together to shop and enjoy the community with neighbors and visitors alike.

GOLDEN1 CREDIT UNION

golden1.com

Golden 1 Credit Union is California's leading financial cooperative and the sixth largest credit union in the U.S.

SOUTH

weheartfriedchicken.com

Located at 2005 11th St. in Southside Park, South is contemporary Southern cuisine, heavy on seasonal vegetables and driven by historical inspiration. South is traditional family food, unpretentious, with no gimmicks, and no crazy science. At South we are not trying to reinvent the wheel, we are just trying to express 200 years of our family's story on a 12" plate.

SIERRA NEVADA DRAUGHT HOUSE

sierranevada.com

The Sierra Nevada Draught House features two bars beautifully designed in reclaimed wood and steel, while the view is second to none. The bar also has two banquets overlooking the interior of the arena bowl and various drink rails throughout the space, perfect for a casual standing reception. Sierra Nevada Brewing Company was founded in Chico, California in 1980.

DOWNTOWN COMMONS (DOCO)

docosacramento.com

It's a night on the town with best friends or a seat in the plaza with coffee and a sketchpad. Seeing your favorite band for the first time. Sitting outside in the warm air with a craft cocktail. Surrounding yourself in amazing art and architecture. Staying at one of the most eclectic hotels in California. Shopping at one-of-a-kind boutiques alongside the most recognized global brands. DOCO is where the locals hang out and visitors from around the globe experience this region at its finest. Sacramento is the next Great American City…and DOCO is our common ground.

DOCO is where the locals hang out and visitors from around the globe experience this region at its finest. Sacramento is the next Great American City and DOCO is our common ground.

GINGER ELIZABETH CHOCOLATES
gingerelizabeth.com
Ginger Elizabeth Chocolates is a Northern California chocolate boutique specializing in chocolate bonbons, macarons and ice cream.

SACRAMENTO INTERNATIONAL AIRPORT
sacramento.aero/smf
With easy freeway access, convenient parking, and the most flyer-friendly experience, Sacramento International Airport makes every journey as easy as SMF.

CALIFORNIA STATE UNIVERSITY, SACRAMENTO

csus.edu

Sacramento State is at the forefront of issues paramount to the region, such as environmental research, politics, business, arts, healthcare, entrepreneurship and more. The University is preparing tomorrow's leaders to embrace California's opportunities, solve its challenges, and redefine what's possible.

It offers 28 post-baccalaureate certificates and 10 credential programs, and houses numerous research and community service centers. It is also the fourth most diverse university in the western United States, according to U.S. News and World Report (2019 rankings).

CESAR CHAVEZ PLAZA

cityofsacramento.org

Cesar Chavez Plaza, or Cesar Chavez Park, named after César Chávez. For more than a century the downtown square has been a focal point for community activities, including the Farmers' Market, music concerts, and community rallies.

GATHER OAK PARK

gathernights.com

Inspired by the warm California nights and the emerging culture of food in the Sacramento region, GATHER is a monthly food focused event that takes a city block and turns it into a bustling dining room or an empty park and turns it into a magical movie night.

Set in a familiar, but unusual setting; this unique food event includes communal tables for out-door dining, beer, food tents, food trucks, a kids area, and live music all night long. GATHER is a place for people to come together and celebrate the one thing we all want to be a part of: Community.

NORTH NATOMAS REGIONAL PARK

cityofsacramento.org

This 212.31 acre park has the several amenities such as softball fields, large and small dog parks with, farmer's market, picnic area, playground, water spray area, and a stage with lawn amphitheater.

ASHA URBAN BATHS

ashaurbanbaths.com

A center for healing and rejuvenation; a gathering place to restore wellbeing with heat and water. Steam room, sauna, warm saltwater soaking pool, cold plunge and lounge--a modern, cultural fusion of the old-world bathhouse.

CALIFORNIA STATE FAIR

calexpostatefair.com

Cal Expo is home to the California State Fair and plays host to hundreds of other signature events each year. Featuring 350 beautifully landscaped acres, Cal Expo was initiated by Governor Pat Brown and opened by Governor Ronald Reagan in 1968. The current Cal Expo facilities were dedicated as a place to celebrate California's achievements, agriculture, diversity of its people, traditions and trends that will shape the Golden State's future.

The California Exposition & State Fair mission is to create a State Fair experience reflecting California including its industries, agriculture, and diversity of its people, traditions and trends shaping its future supported by year-round events.

RARETEA

rareteausa.com

Established in Berkeley, California in 2016 under the name TeaOne. Since then it has opened multiple branches across Northern California. In June 2018, TeaOne opened is first oversea branch in Guangzhou, China. So far, RareTea is a well-known and popular boba tea brand in Northern California with a massive fan base in UC Berkeley and UC Davis. As a result, the University of California had invited our brand to open multiple locations inside the two universities.